THE FIRST TIME

TRUE STORIES VOLUME 2

WHAT THEY SAID ABOUT THE ORIGINAL QUEBEC EDITION OF THIS SERIES

Tender and funny. La Première Fois *is the kind of book that school libraries should display on their most prominent shelves. It will be a lot more helpful than condom-vending machines.*

— Le Soleil

A lot of myths are dispelled. First attempts are not always glorious, and this is precisely what teenagers will enjoy recognizing in these stories.

— Le Devoir

Magnificent. An occasion for young and old to share on an important transition. Get hold of these gems!

— Des livres et des jeunes

True and sincere (and, one might add, indispensable for adolescents). A must-read!

— Lurelu

Marvelous. An absolute masterpiece.

— En Toutes Lettres (CBC Radio)

Touching and well-rendered. Today's teens will totally identify with these tales.

— Ici comme ailleurs (CBC Radio)

These are books for intelligent readers. La Première Fois *can help parents understand how their kids cope with their brand new sexual itches.*

— Nuit blanche

A molotov cocktail in the field of children's literature. Well-written and well-balanced, with a variety of sexual options. A daring première indeed.

— Le Droit

A "WHITE RAVEN" OF THE INTERNATIONAL YOUTH LIBRARY, MUNICH

(a selection of the world's best books for young people)

THE FIRST TIME

TRUE STORIES VOLUME 2

BRIAN DOYLE
LEANNE FRANSON
LINDA M. BRISSETT
W.P. KINSELLA
MARTIN STEPHENS
JILL GOLICK
CHARLES MONTPETIT
JULIE LAWSON

edited by CHARLES MONTPETIT

ORCA BOOK PUBLISHERS

Canadian Cataloguing in Publication Data

Main entry under title:
The first time

ISBN 1-55143-037-1 (v. 1) – ISBN 1-55143-039-8 (v. 2)

1. Youth – Sexual behavior. 2. Premarital sex. I. Montpetit, Charles, 1958 -

HQ27.F57 1995 306.77'00835 C95–910447–X

Publication assistance by The Canada Council

Cover design by Suburbia Studios

Printed and bound in Canada

Orca Book Publishers
PO Box 5626, Station B
Victoria, BC Canada
V8R 6S4

Orca Book Publishers
PO Box 468
Custer, WA USA
98240-0468

10 9 8 7 6 5 4 3 2 1

CONTENTS

PRECAUTIONS

(A summary of the introduction that appeared in Volume 1)

While the following stories are true, they're not necessarily autobiographical, even if they are written in the first person. They shouldn't be interpreted as model experiences, either: we're merely passing on how real people acted and felt in specific circumstances – mistakes and all.

The pictures, however, really are from the authors' youths. Call it a gesture of solidarity with our characters if you will, but we just thought it was a fun idea.

Need we add that these are very subjective accounts? Of course, all the possible angles could not be covered herein, and we can't guarantee that the experiences we did write about represent an accurate cross-section of society. But we do hope that these tales will move and entertain you.

RECORDER LESSON

BRIAN DOYLE

It's hard to believe that Brian Doyle still considers himself an "amateur" as far as writing is concerned. After all, his name, voice and style are amongst the most widely recognized in the field of young adult literature. His novels *Up to Low* and *Easy Avenue* both won the Canadian Library Association Book of the Year Award, while *Covered Bridge* got the Mr. Christie Book Award for English text and his entire production earned the Vicky Metcalf Award for a body of work. Now, really, is that the track record of an amateur?

Still, if he feels that the thirty years he

spent as a teacher in the Ottawa Valley take precedence over his career as an author, who are we to argue? What's important is that Brian does what he does from the heart, and gets deeply involved in just about everything he undertakes – his books, for instance, are all solidly grounded in personal lore, whether they are about his family, himself or close acquaintances.

But if you believe that the following story was easy for him to write, think again. Our invitation stirred up a lot of buried emotions, and we came this close to losing him during the period over which the project was built. It just goes to show that there's more to a First Time than meets the eye, even when an episode sounds like a perfect fantasy.

Enjoy.

Recorder Lesson

I played the recorder.

I had a job at the Ottawa exhibition in the summer of 1947 playing the recorder outside our church's bingo tent.

The recorder music was to attract people to the tent to take a closer look at the cute guy with the curly hair playing the recorder, whose curls and charming music would somehow seduce them into buying a bingo card or two.

Across from the church bingo tent was the beginning of the midway and the "girlie show," as it was called.

Beyond that was the Alligator Man, whose skin was so thick he invited audience volunteers to come up and try to cut through the soles of his feet with a hacksaw.

Next to that was a show with huge billboards outside with crude paintings of different kinds of torture. A head sticking out of the sand with ants eating its eyes and tongue. Inside, however, was just a wax-museum type of display – lights flashing, phony screams of horror and a curtain that cost an extra dime to go through, where you saw a bloodied head on a platter.

Next was the fantastic boy who was "brought up by reptiles." For fifteen cents you could go in and watch a guy crawl around in the mud.

Down toward the end of the midway was the "Siamese Triplets Inside" show. The paintings showed three children, attached at the hips and heads, dancing with little umbrellas on a stage with a huge symphony orchestra and acrobats and monkeys and clowns. Inside, you got a dark passageway, strange music and then a little stage area lighting up a big jar. Inside the jar, floating, was a membrane or something; maybe it was a dead jellyfish, or just a couple of pieces of rubber; perhaps – it was hard to tell.

Back to the girlie show at my end of the midway.

Every hour a drummer, a saxophone and a trumpet would come out on the deck in front of the girlie show tent, and a loud guy on a vicious microphone would give you a piece of the action that you would see inside if you bought a ticket.

While the music blared and the microphone blasted, out would come half a dozen dancers in high heels and wiggly little skimpy outfits, with bells on their ankles and feathers on their wrists and piled-up hair.

It was hard to play the recorder while this was going on. Not only would I be completely drowned out, but my imagination was so inflamed by the sight of all that wiggling, jiggling, bouncing girlie flesh that I couldn't get the recorder to do what I could normally make it do.

My boss at the bingo tent was concerned that I would be corrupted by this sinful display. She was a friend of my mother's and the main reason I got the job. My mother must have asked her to keep an eye on me. She must have told her that I was at a very susceptible age. My mother would do that kind of thing. That is why my boss would leave her bingo duties and come out and protect me from the girlie show whenever it appeared on the platform.

Her way of screening me from being sucked into a sewer of sex forever was to get me to play louder on the recorder.

If you've ever played the recorder, you'll know that you can't play *louder* on the instrument. A recorder must be played with gentle breath. You can't force your breath on a recorder and make it louder.

But my boss would stand there and urge

me on to compete with the band and the screeching microphone.

"Louder! Louder!" she'd shout. "Keep playing! Keep playing!"

The hymn "Abide With Me" was what I usually played during this time.

One hot afternoon I noticed that the girlie on the end of the line of jigglers had me rivetted with her eyes. Once she was sure I was watching, she gave a couple of extra twirls to the twirlers on her breasts and fluttered the flat of her hand at me and then ground her pelvis and bumped her crotch and flashed me a big wink and a delicious smile.

"Louder. Louder!" shouted my mother's friend, as I played "Abide With Me," the hymn that asks God to stick by you even as the darkness thickens.

Next to the girlie show tent was a trailer where the dancers changed costumes between acts. They would exit the trailer down three steps and pick their way daintily over ropes and pegs until they disappeared behind the tent.

And then I could see them run back when their dance was finished, bangles and beads bouncing, bells jingling, heels clacking, breasts and bums pushing and straining the shimmering fabric of their tiny outfits.

"Keep playing," my mother's friend would

hiss behind me, as she passed conveniently by with a handful of bingo cards.

This particular day, as the girls left the trailer to go backstage, the last one, the one who'd been giving me all the attention, shouted "Nice piccolo!" and then twitched her ass at me, a gesture that nearly knocked me off my chair.

At the end of the act, instead of following the others into the trailer, she cut across and, to my disbelief, came up to my chair.

She stood with the August sun behind her, bathed in gold, her form shimmering, her perfume washing over me in a glorious vapour.

I see this scene yet, after all these years, frozen in time.

She leaned and placed her lips to my ear.

"Could you teach me to work that piccolo?" she whispered, causing a ripple of goose flesh to run down my spine, playing it like a xylophone.

"It's not a piccolo, it's a recorder," I said, turning my head slightly until our eyes met.

"Whatever it is," she said, "you could show me . . . " She blew a little burst of breath into my ear.

As I drowned in her eyes, the voice of my protector stiffened me up.

"Excuse me!" she boomed. "Is there something I can do for you, young lady?"

"My name is Nan," said the lips at my ear. "My supper break is at six. Meet me behind the trailer."

"Pardon me, miss," persisted my boss. "I think you'd better clear out of here and go about your business!"

Nan gave my hand and my recorder a squeeze.

Then she clicked away in a little hurricane of perfume and feathers.

I could see that my mother's friend was about to make a speech so I put my recorder to my lips and played "Abide With Me" until she gave up and left.

It was the best I'd ever played it, trills and all. Since we were in a quiet time, I thought maybe Nan would hear it while she stripped off her costume in the darkened trailer.

At six o'clock, while my boss was down the midway buying hamburgers, I walked across, shoving the recorder into my pocket to disguise the lump in my pants.

She was sitting on a bench behind the trailer, holding a mirror, trimming her hair. She wore a red satin kimono decorated with designs of musical instruments in black thread.

Around her, the cables and tarps and boxes and discarded makeup packs and usual backstage litter took on a prettiness in the early evening light.

The shouts of the children on the distant rides and the rumble of the grinding machinery reached our privacy, muffled, from another world.

The hint in the air of candy floss, hemp and canvas was sexual.

It still is, to me.

"Would you like to come in?" she said. "The rest are away at supper."

She took me by the hand and led me up the three steps into the trailer.

There, in the gloom, I could make out two narrow cots, rows of costumes on hangers, a long mirror with lights over it, four stools, a small, dirty window, a little table.

"Would you help me with something?" she said, sitting on the first cot.

"I'm trimming my hair down here," she said, opening her kimono and stretching her legs straight out. "It's hard to see," she said. "Could you do some for me?"

She handed me the scissors and opened her legs wide and leaned back on her elbows and smiled a beautiful smile.

I didn't move.

My eyes were used to the light now.

I'd never seen a naked woman before.

She seemed sweetly, mildly amused.

"Is that your piccolo in your pocket?" she said. "Mmm?"

"It's a recorder," I said.

"Oh yes, recorder," she said. "May I see it?"

I removed the recorder from my pocket and handed it to her, my hands shaking.

"You're not going to be able to give me a trim shaking like that. Come here." She pouted, like a mother about to readjust her kid's clothing for him.

She took the scissors from me and placed them on the little table.

She undid my belt and unzipped my fly and pulled down my pants and underwear.

"Is this your first time?" she said.

"Yes," I said, my voice hardly working.

She handed back the recorder.

"Show me how you play," she said.

As I put the recorder to my lips she shifted on the cot and leaned into me and gently fed me into her mouth.

I began to play "Abide With Me."

Out the little window I could see my boss, my mother's friend, standing in front of the bingo tent, holding hamburgers, cocking her ear, listening. Was that a recorder she could hear, faint, faltering, hesitating, then fading plaintively . . . ?

That night I looked in my bedroom mirror deep into my face, searching for any kind of change that I might have undergone. I saw none.

The next day, Monday, I was shocked to see a whole new girlie show move in. A big sign went up:

ALL NEW GIRLIE SHOW!

I sat in my chair in front of the bingo tent and glumly watched the new dancers come out on the stage to the blaring music.

They looked old and bored.

"Where'd you get to last night?" my boss asked me. "I had your supper for you and you never showed up."

"Sorry," I said. "I forgot."

"And why aren't you playing?" she said.

"Can't find my piccolo," I said.

The new dancer on the end had skinny legs and bony knees. Her face looked like she was in some kind of pain.

"Piccolo? You mean recorder! What happened to your recorder?"

"I lost it," I said, and went home.

I often think of Nan, even after all these years.

I wonder if she ever used the basic fingering I showed her.

I wonder if she still has my recorder.

I wonder if she ever thinks of me.

IMPECCABLE TASTE

LEANNE FRANSON

She hates it when people point it out, but it's still true: Leanne Franson doesn't look her age. If you take a quick look at this Saskatchewan-born waif with torn clothes and one hell of an attitude, you'll never guess that she's currently published in three different countries, from glossy anthologies to innumerable periodicals – none of which she dares show her grandmother.

The authoritative *Comics Journal* has labelled her work "amazingly expressive," "almost magical" and a "pure pleasure." In the U.S., her material alongside that of cartoon legends,

Nicole Hollander, Roberta Gregory and Alison Bechdel. And when we contacted her, she was involved in no less than four projects for children and teens, plus a serial and the ongoing publication of her own Liliane comic books, the U.K. edition of which had just been released by the London Cartoon Centre.

Yet she found the time to adapt an episode of her heroine's real-life adventures for us. Needless to say, we're *damn* proud to have her on board.

I always did have impeccable taste in men:
...hey Mona!! ...i met a new guy!!
...so what's wrong with him? ...married like Bob... or at least engaged?... ...is he moving to Spain?... or China, maybe?
hah!
HAIRDO
...in fact he's PERFECT!! ...he's gorgeous and artsy and he'll even dance when he's not drunk!!
But my lustful fantasies were not to be fulfilled...
...i knew it!!
...the only non-neanderthal male in the whole PROVINCE and he writes to say he's HOMOSEXUAL!!
what to do but swallow my sexual pride?...
...of course i accept you as you are David. ...i'm touched you told me.
With time David became my confidant and i, his.
...and then Jason's sister got up to pee and we hid behind the T.V. ...
why does he have to be gay!! drat!

By the time Mona and i moved to Montréal for University...
...i hope college men are less stupid...
...i wonder if anyone will speak english?
... i had become very gay-positive.
FUCKIN' FAGGOTS!!
...only faggots can call faggots faggots!
...my first week of classes i was SLIGHTLY nervous...
...everyone here is so cool... i'm sure they all draw better than i can...
...but willing to be distracted:
...wow! what a bod!!
...and he's in my class yet!! ...got talent too!!
Not knowing anyone in Montréal except Mona gave me an excuse to follow him home...

...liliane! what a surprise!
hiya!! mind if i eat my lunch with you?
...not at all!...but before we go upstairs i've got to tell you something...
it'll depend on how open-minded you are...
...he's either gay, or a drug dealer!!
...i'm gay...
My impeccable taste had struck again!
...boy, will Mona be surprised.
I was becoming an expert at channelling my sexual energy...
...god, i wish i were a gay boy...
...at least i'm learning French!
300 illustrations en noir et blanc..
AMOUR GAI
LES PLAISIRS DE L'AMOUR GAI
...and Pierre got me into other ways of being physical:

From time to time we discussed my sexuality:
...i still think you're really hot, Pierre...
...aren't you ever attracted to other women?
...sure i've thought about it... but i've also thought about walking on the moon ...
...in fact i wasn't much attracted to women's company at all...
...the women's center is having a dance on Friday... ...wanna go?
oh boy!
ya know, Mona... given a room with men on one side and women on the other...
...if i started out with the women, i'd end up with the men...
...right. ...well, come to the dance and see.
i was very sure of myself.
I was willing to humor an old friend... to a point.
...sure i'll go to the gay filmfest with you, Pierre... it'll give me a good excuse to leave Mona's dance early!

The night of the dance i was REALLY looking forward to that film:...
i can't believe i'm here!!
...you'll live.
...but the mood was infectious:
...my god! ...i'm having fun!... i almost don't miss the guys!
...in fact, it's a real relief not getting cruised!! ...you can really let go!!
That dance turned out to be educational in more than one way:
...they're lesbians ...
I'd only seen women together in "men's" magazines before ... and they certainly weren't LESBIANS...
...i wonder if real lesbians hate men...
... and i thought it was a bad stereotype that they wear men's suits...
hey, cinderella! ... time for you to get going!

I was still preoccupied at the movie...
...i can't believe i only know gay men ... no gay women...
...which was definitely a change of pace from that dance...
...great jerk-off film, eh, liliane!
...you know, Pierre... i'd never tell Mona, but i actually regret leaving that dance!
See ya tomorrow?
...uh... i gotta tell you some-thing, liliane...
...i can't see you outside of school anymore... my boyfriend is jealous...
...he thinks you're trying to steal me... i don't want to lose him.

Mona wasn't much comfort ...
That's men for you.
... and then i lost her too!
... i got accepted at the University of Toronto this fall!!
That September i was a pitiful sight indeed.
... no fag friend, no room-mate ... what am i gonna do?
Then one day i bumped into one of Mona's friends:
... hiya liliane! You look a bit down! ... miss Mona, eh ... well, come with me to the women's center if you're not busy right now...
Feeling too apathetic to refuse...
... god, i'll never live this down if Mona finds out!
You'll love the women's center!
... i tagged along...
HERSTORY
WITCHES
NOT A BABY
FEMINIST THEORY
KNOW YOUR BODY
WOMEN WRITE
GYN
lesbian
VOTE
... oh my god!! ... a feminist hell-hole!

Just then...
...this had never happened to me before... at least never with... a... WOMAN!
BLOOP!
I heard absolutely nothing of that general meeting...
...i'm clea, and i'm in Social sciences ...
... or ALMOST nothing!
...my name is Mikki... ...and i'm a LESBIAN and PROUD of it!
I was torn between running from the room screaming, and kneeling to kiss her feet...
...oh my god!!... a lesbian!... oh! ...how can i feel like this?! ...oh... i'm so confused!
PATHUMP..PATHUMP..PATHUMP......PATHUMP...PATHUMP...PATHUM
...the first meeting of the "Caucus on Lesbianism" is tomorrow evening at seven ...

...then i decided that this panic was definitely lesbophobic!
...this is ridiculous! ...gay men don't phase me!
PA...THUMP.. PA..THUMP...
Gathering up my courage, i faced my fears...
...uh... mikki?!
?
...uh, hi!! ...uh, i'm, uh.. straight, but i wondered if, uh, well, if you'd feel uncomfortable with a straight woman at your meeting tomorrow... i mean, i'd understand if you...
...no, it'd be GREAT if you could come...
poor girl
Boy would Mona be surprised
...but after all, it's just for research ...isn't it?
There i was the next evening, feeling much the voyeur...
...all these women are lesbians! ...what if they knew i'm straight?!

...until my thoughts were interrupted: Mikki had the floor...
...we've got to raise awareness on campus! ...last year i organised a women's health fair in residence
...and my heart.
...and no one came...
...how could life be so cruel to poor Mikki? ...i wanna hold her in my arms and make everything alright!
Were these appropriate thoughts for a straight woman... even one battling lesbophobia?
...she's so beautiful... But why am i thinking that? ...why do i keep forgetting that i'm straight?!
...Hey! Let's get this meeting over with! Who's going out dancing tonight?!
...GEE! ...dancing not only with WOMEN like last year... but with lesbians!! ...i wonder if i should?!
...comin' dancing, liliane? ...i'd personally like you to come...
dancing with Mikki!

...uh.. yeah!
...she wants me to come! "Personally"!!
...poor girl thinks she's straight!
... we've got a coupla hours... wanna eat at my place? ... i've just got to stop off at a store...
alone with ♡ ♡ Mikki!
Did i want to?! I would've followed her anywhere!
...do you like yogurt? ...broccoli?
my favorites!
...what charm! What romance! What straight woman wouldn't have fallen... and fallen hard?!
...i hope you don't mind eating the broccoli raw with your fingers... my room-mate didn't do the dishes and the stove is broken...
she's so suave!!
...all too soon this intimate interlude was over...
...time to head to the bar to meet the others...
...guess we're early!
...wow! ...a lesbian bar!
D.J. is OUT

...we'll just wait here for the others...
...this isn't so scary...
...i'm so glad you decided to come...
...you know, i really like how you dress...
...oh my god! She's holding my hand! A lesbian is holding my hand!
...yeah, i really like you...
...wow!...another woman's hand!! ...it's so small... so much like mine! Her skin is so soft!
...what gorgeous eyes...

what gorgeous lips...
...this is really happening !!
...wow... ...a woman... ...sigh
Hey you two!! Are you gonna sit there all night?
...all that panic!...and then it felt so natural!
...coming to join me?

... dance!!! hell!! ... i was flying!
... oh Mikki Mikki Mikki Mikki!!!
That night i floated home...
... Mikki really likes me!! ... she likes me, she likes me, she really does like me!
... and sleep was a long time coming.
... i kissed Mikki!! ... it felt so natural! ... and i'm gonna see her again!! ...
The next day at school i was not quite there...
... something's up! She hasn't drawn a thing all class!
... I think i'll tell Pierre!! ... won't HE ever be surprised!

...here it comes!
Hey Pierre...
... i think i'm in love...
... with a WOMAN!!!
I was waitin' for it!
hmph!! ... some surprise.
... i KNEW it!
... i know!! ... i'll call Mona long-distance tonight! ... she'll be surprised!!
After school, just walking through the streets was an entirely new experience.
... wow! ... women!
... at home:
... hey Mona!! ... i'm in love with a lesbian!

...after all that "don't like silly women" shit...
...i suppose i should be surprised... but frankly, i'm not AT ALL!
CLICK!
Next:
...Hey David! Long time no talk to!... Guess what?... i met a woman...
...and now you're calling me up to say you're in love!
How'd you guess!
...come on, liliane. I saw it coming YEARS ago!! Besides Chloë discovered women in Montréal this summer too!
Time to resort to drastic measures!
Hi, Mom...
...Well, liliane... i'm glad you're not telling me this at 15, but you know by now i trust your judgment. You're a grown woman now...

...how come the only one really surprised was myself... ...was i really that blind to myself and that transparent to everyone else? What of all the famous rejection?
...the shock and disbelief?
...the oppression and outrage?
I conveniently forgot to call my Dad, and started worrying about more pressing matters:
...i wonder if i'll have sex with Mikki? Lesbians have got to be better for my sex life than gay men!... am i a lesbian too if i sleep with her?
As far as sex was concerned i was no neophyte... but this was new terrain:
...let's see... i am always lecturing hets on gay male sex... kissing'll be the same as with men... less facial hair... she'll have breasts...
...it'll be like masturbating myself, i guess... and then there's ORAL SEX!!
... i always expect guys to go down on me, so i guess she may expect me to... let's see... it would probably taste like me, or close...
ZiPP!!
SNIFF SNIFF SNIFF
...hmmmm...

...i know!! ... i'll practice like i did with french-kissing when i was 14 ... On my hand!
That night i happily set to work ... with BOTH my hands!
oh! liliane!!
The next evening my date with Mikki turned out to be 3/4 of a double-date:
... this is Millie... she's the one who brought me out in May...
Nonetheless i met cool people, heard new music...
...what a wild party! Everyone's wearing black!
...and learnt all about non-monogamy.
...yeah, Millie was my first lover. She's really political... she says that monogamy is a patriarchal plot to control us.
...being a lesbian sure is complicated!
But as for my sex-life... I did as well with Pierre!
... Millie and i just got offered a ride ... see ya soon, liliane!
Shit!

Next week, another date...
La Rue! La Nuit! Femmes Sans Peur!!
À BAS LE VIOL!
NO MEANS NO!!
this feminist stuff is almost fun!!
and this time, a sleep-over!
LA RUE! LA NUIT FEMMES SANS PEUR!
...you can stay with me at Millie's... The dance after this will end real late...
here's my chance!
NO MEANS NO
But although Mikki and Millie were no longer "together", i was the one who ended up alone...
So much for practicing on my hand! For what!
Giggle... Giggle... Giggle...
In the morning there did still appear to be some hope...
...you know, liliane, i love you more than anyone except Millie...
...and i know how much she loves millie...
Pop!
T 2
...gullible!
...in my kitchen, yet!
...i wonder if she still thinks she's straight?
...She loves me!!
...with a few minor humiliations on the way.
HEY MILLIE!! Liliane's on the Pill!!
...not anymore!!

Finally some time away from Millie!
...i gotta pick up some stuff from where i used to stay and take it to my new place if you wanna come...
...yeah, my first year here i had a nervous breakdown: i didn't know i was a lesbian...
I couldn't wait for something to change my status:
...never slept with a woman, and you wanna call yourself a lesbian?!
...in love with a woman and you're straight?!
Back at her new place:
...women are so cute when they're first coming out...
...this is getting easier all the time!
...maybe i wasn't straight!
...maybe i wasn't straight!
...you're pretty aggressive with women for a straight girl, liliane...
...i really am, aren't i!
While she showered i only had one thing in mind...
...are we going to do it?!
...am i really a lesbian too?
...wow! me and another woman! ...sex with Mikki!
...sex with Mikki!

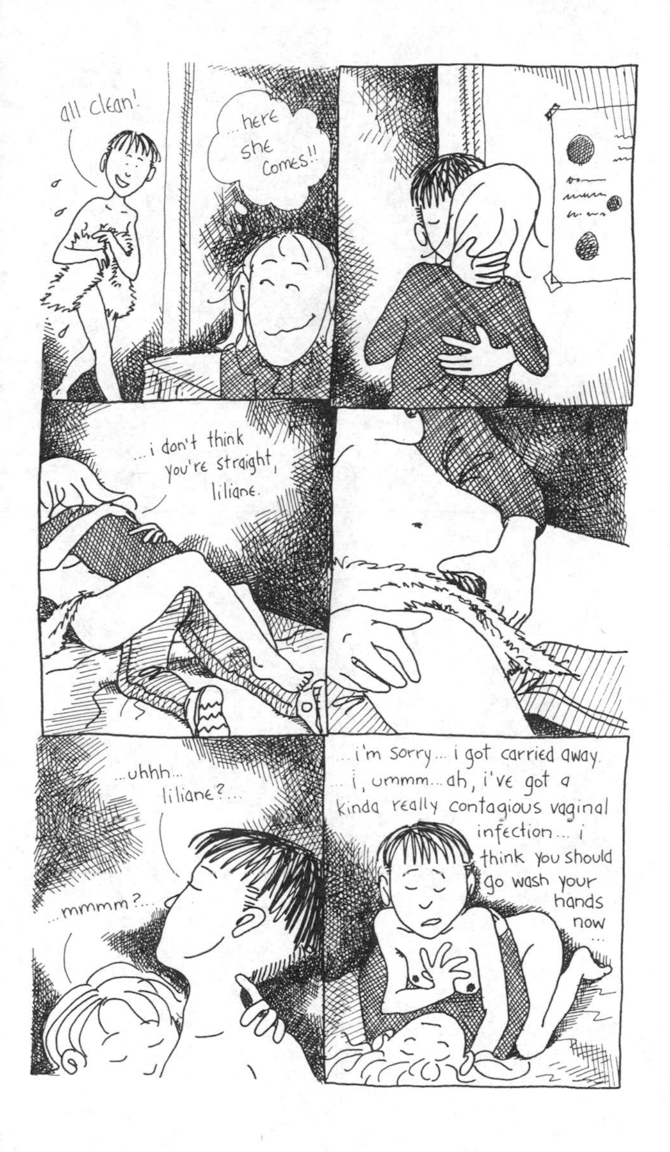
all clean!
...here she comes!!
...i don't think you're straight, liliane.
...uhhh... liliane?...
...mmmm?...
...i'm sorry... i got carried away. ...i, ummm...ah, i've got a kinda really contagious vaginal infection... i think you should go wash your hands now ...

...sigh
...Millicent?... yah, we'll come for dinner... ...uh, huh... she's here now... ...huh?
Walls in old Montréal apartments are very thin:
...i really do wanna sleep with her... but i love YOU, millie!! i know... ...but still...
... i gotta get dressed... we're invited to dinner at Millie's...
I was very quiet on the way to Millie's...
...i don't think i like non-monogamy
...you know... i want to still be with Millie when i'm eighty...
I ran blindly into the first available arms:
?!
...i can't stand this!!
?!
!

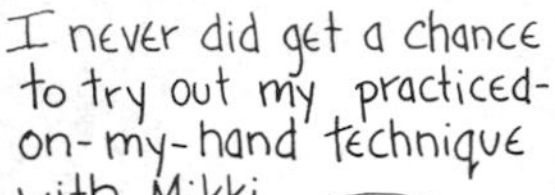
I never did get a chance to try out my practiced-on-my-hand technique with Mikki...

...now WHY did i think lesbians would be better for my sex life than gay men?...

...in fact we never even kissed again.

My love and desire for her didn't die quickly...
...maybe if i write and tell her how i feel, she'll...

... although i eventually moved on.
2nd Anniversary!! liliane and Sophie

But back then i discovered...
...you look a bit down, liliane...

...that my taste in love objects was still... impeccable.
I'm in love with Mikki..
...yeah, me too! ...but she's in love with Millie.

INNOCENCE AND PASSION

LINDA M. BRISSETT

After completing a course in Creative Writing and Journalism, Jamaican-born Linda M. Brissett has had several articles and two books of poems published in the United States and Canada. But, as a Hamilton nurse who has specialised in intensive care for premature and sick babies for twenty-eight years, she's also had firsthand experience with the traumas, the confusion and, sometimes, the tragedies that can be caused by inadequate information on human sexuality.

"Not only did I learn in great detail about the structures and functions of human sex organs," says she, "but as part of my practicum, I had to examine and handle them, and do it objectively." Before long, she became comfortable with the most intimate medical procedures, and during her travels, she had plenty of opportunities to advise people about sexual matters.

The story she wrote for us, however, is *not* one of those level-headed lectures. In fact, it's quite the opposite, for Linda is talking here about that rarest of emotion – the love-at-first-sight thunderbolt. If you think you can stay rational through such a storm, you're in for one heckuva of a surprise.

Innocence and Passion

The golden rays of the sun fired the August evening with heaping coals of flames. All around me, the sleepy waters of the Ribbon River reflected the blazing scenery.

I jumped from the last boulder, onto the path that sprouted out of the riverbed. My toes dug into the trodden vegetation, and the notepad and pencil in my skirt pocket began to tap rhythmically against my thigh as I climbed up the embankment.

Just when I could see the row of trees that marked our backyard boundary, he appeared out of nowhere. I jumped back.

"You scared me half to death," I shouted. Yet I was not quite sure if my racing heartbeat was a result of fright, or some other strange stirrings within myself.

He stood with arms akimbo, looking down at me, grinning from ear to ear.

"I'm sorry," he said, and sounded as

though he meant it. "I didn't intend to frighten you. I just wanted to see you again, and maybe talk a little bit."

He pulled a blade of fever grass from a clump that was growing nearby and started stripping it absentmindedly, his gaze attached to my own. I averted my eyes for a moment, and looked beyond him to the sky and the trees. A lone John Crow sat atop a coconut palm, enjoying the latent rays of the setting sun.

When I looked back at him, he was staring at my feet.

"I'm always barefooted when I go down to write by the river," I said defensively. I found it difficult to speak above the pounding of my heart.

"I know that," he replied softly, as if he was trying to pacify me. "I watched you yesterday, and the day before. I was sitting behind that tree over there so you wouldn't see me."

"You were spying on me?" My uneasiness gave way to consternation and annoyance. What if I had gone skinny-dipping, as I often did when it was hot? I blushed with belated embarrassment.

He moved slowly toward me, and took both my hands in his. "I just wanted to be near you, but I wasn't sure you'd let me. What do you write? Verses and stuff, I bet."

"Yes," I whispered, and as he pulled me closer to him, his eager lips found mine.

Waves of emotion crashed over me, wrenching me out to sea. I could not explain it, but they brought out such feelings, I wished they'd last and last. Not only was I responding, I was thoroughly enjoying it.

Had I completely lost my mind? Here I was in the bushes, locked in the arms of a total stranger who was trying his best to pull my tongue from its root! What if Mom came down the path this moment, though? What would she do to me?

Mom was a wonderful and caring woman, but she was very old-fashioned when it came to sex. She never spoke openly about it. On many occasions, she even showed outright disapproval when our neighbours' dogs jumped each other and became "fastened." She'd send me into the house so I wouldn't see the spectacle, then she'd try to separate the animals with whatever was on hand, be it a broom or a garden hose.

She was a stenographer for Denoes & Lever, a modest-sized law firm in the town of Vere, Manchester, about five miles from our prefab bungalow home. The distance did not seem to daunt her. Sometimes she would walk to and from work when her old Morris Minor was in the garage for repairs, which was often.

Dad, on the other hand, had recently been offered a post teaching the eighth grade at a newly opened private school in Santa Cruz, fifty miles away. Since it was too far away for him to commute, and since Mom did not want to give up her position or move house, they agreed that he would board with his headmaster's family, and come home every Friday evening.

I remember the first weekend Dad returned from Santa Cruz. I had run into his arms, hoping that he would tell me all about his work. But after a quick hug, and a promise that we would talk after he had rested up, he had disappeared into the bedroom, with Mom right on his heels. They had not emerged from their hideout for over an hour, and when they did, neither of them looked any more rested. It took eighteen months of similar Friday-evening rituals before I discovered what it was all about.

It was the day before my fourteenth birthday, and I had arrived home late from a softball match. Dad's Hillman Minx was parked at the gate, and Mom's Morris was in the carport. I was glad they had gotten home earlier than I. At least they would have had their rest, and would be ready to spend some time with me.

I jumped onto the veranda, eager to see if they had awakened. The jalousie window in their bedroom overlooked the front yard, and the blinds were opened enough for me to see into the room. I peered in, and froze in shock.

Dad and Mom were stark naked, thrashing around on the floor, their clothes strewn about them. I could not see Mom's face, but her ebony legs were wrapped around Dad's neck, while his buttocks moved rhythmically, in and out, under her. I stifled the urge to scream, but in spite of my attempts to remain unnoticed, I must have made some noise, because Dad stiffened and turned toward the window. I leapt off the veranda and ran down to the river.

The river had been my source of inspiration ever since I started writing: once again I turned to it for comfort and serenity. The incident had left me angry, confused and ashamed. For years, my mother's attitude had taught me that sexual intercourse was utterly disgraceful. Yet both she and Dad had obviously been enjoying themselves. How hypocritical!

I doused my mixed-up feelings in the cold water, then returned home and pretended nothing was wrong. But when I finally went to bed that night, I heard my parents whispering in the other room, wondering if I had caught them in the act.

"You must talk to her about this, Doris," my father said. "She's old enough to know the facts of life, and you are babying her. You should have dealt with it more thoroughly when she started menstruating."

I wondered why Dad had not told me himself, since he felt so strongly about it. After all, he was my parent, too. But as was his way, he left it up to Mom. She promised him that she would speak to me the next day.

She never did. What I eventually learned, I got from my friends, like Irene Folkes, who had been sexually active since she was twelve. Still, I remained inhibited and shy around boys for a long time.

That is, until last week.

"Sybil! Sybil DeCambre! Over here, my dear."

Mom and I were doing our Saturday shopping in Solas Market when she spotted a familiar face in the crowd. I quickly gathered the oranges that Ms. Rosa had just handed to me, so we could greet the newcomers without holding up the line.

"That must be her nephew from Kingston," said Mom in conspiratorial tones. "I hear he's a very bright boy—wants to be a doctor. Hi, Sybil!" I looked up and saw that Ms. DeCambre stood next to a tall, young man about my age, maybe seventeen. He was dark-complexioned, with short, wavy hair parted on the left. His eyes slanted slightly upward like mine, and emphasized his handsome, oval face. His white T-shirt hung loosely over khaki shorts, but what grabbed my attention about him was his smooth, almost liquid gait, and the obvious strength of his arms and legs. He must have been an athlete – a runner: strong, fast and agile.

"... my nephew, Kenneth Dunklay. Ken, this is Doris Nethersole, and her lovely daughter Vearda. They are our neighbours."

"How do you do?" He shook Mom's hand and then mine, flashing the most beautiful smile I had seen on anyone's face. His handshake caused instant combustion, and the heat engulfed my whole body.

"Ken is staying with us for a few weeks," Ms. DeCambre announced. "It will be nice to have a child in our house again."

A child, I thought. *He's hardly a child – no child can make me feel the way he's making me feel.*

"I came up yesterday for a holiday," he added after I reluctantly took back my hand. "My parents are on a business trip to Cayman Brac, so it was a good time for me to visit my aunt and uncle." He wouldn't take his eyes off me. "And I certainly hope to see more of *you.*"

"Of course you will," said Ms. DeCambre with a knowing smile. "You'll show Ken around the district, won't you, Vearda?"

"Yes, I guess so," I answered meekly.

"Nice meeting you, Ms. Nethersole." He touched my chin with a finger, and walked off with his aunt.

"How about dinner at our house next Friday?" Mom shouted after them.

"That will be fine with us, Doris," Ms. DeCambre shouted back. I stood staring at their receding figures until they were out of sight.

Mom's voice broke into my jumbled thoughts. "He seems a nice lad! I think he's taken a shine to you, Ver."

Her casual manner surprised me. She was not annoyed or angry that this stranger had demonstrated such an obvious interest in me. In fact, she seemed pleased about it.

"Just you be careful if you go out with him," she said. "We don't want you to get pregnant out of wedlock."

In a single sentence, Mom had shattered the magic of the moment.

Our lips still locked in a resounding kiss, he walked me slowly but deliberately off the path and into the bushes. The bauxite-rich earth, soft and inviting, became our temporary bed.

He opened my blouse and started feeling for my breasts. He found them unharnessed. My nipples became pebbles between his eager fingers. I knew I should stop this madness now, but I wasn't prepared for any of this. Caught in a moment of unleashed passion, I was physically unable to think.

A shudder went through me when I realized that he had undone his pants. His erect organ was between my thighs, hard as a bone and probing.

"No!" I tried to say, but couldn't, for his mouth held mine as if forever. His hand slipped under my skirt and pulled in my buttocks. I could feel my panties dangling from my left ankle, but I had no idea when they got there.

I was weak with abandonment, and a million never-felt-before emotions.

Then, the searing pain of the penetration wracked my groin, my thighs, my whole body. All of a sudden, I was pushing against him with all the strength I could muster.

"Ahhhhhh!"

Ken suddenly let go of me and rolled on his back amidst the dampened leaves.

"Oh! I'm cut, oh God, I'm cut!"

He was on his knees now, rocking back and forth in agony. His pants hanging below his buttocks, he gingerly cradled his flaccid penis with both hands. Blood was spurting from its tip. *What in God's name was happening?*

I jumped up, and quickly replaced my undergarment. My inner thighs felt moist and sticky where he had ejaculated, but I was too concerned about Ken to give it a second thought.

"What's the matter?" I asked, suddenly realizing the enormity of the situation.

He pulled his shorts up, carefully avoiding his penis, and loosely buckled his belt. A dark spot slowly started to spread on the front of the pants.

"You cut me," he said. "I've got a hair cut, and it hurts like hell. What am I going to do?"

"I cut you?" I didn't understand what he was talking about. "I did no such thing!"

The feelings that had held me spellbound for a brief while had vanished, leaving me confused, disappointed and fearful.

As if he could read my mind, Ken came to me and hugged me briefly. He seemed more in control of himself now.

"It's not your fault," he said soothingly. "I guess I got cut by one of your pubic hairs, or something. I have to go and get it looked after."

(Years later, I learned that there was a much more plausible explanation for what had actually happened. A man's frenulum – that little piece of tissue which links the foreskin to the glans – sometimes get ruptured when it's too tight to start with. It's a bit like the male counterpart to the breaking of a woman's hymen, only much rarer.)

Ken started hobbling up the path, then turned around, kissed me lightly and said, "It was my first time, too. I love you."

"I love you, too," I whispered, and he walked away.

I returned to the river, thinking of him. He would have to go to the doctor and receive stitches (which he did). His aunt and uncle would know about us. My parents would find out, too! What is my mother going to say? What will she do? What if I became pregnant? I knew I was certainly going to be more prepared in the future.

And then a voice in my head said *To hell with them all*. I immediately felt whole, and free, and wonderful. *I don't care who knows*, I thought. *I don't care if everybody knows. I love Ken and he loves me.* I experienced no shame, just joy.

"Joy!" I shouted as I ran down the path.

The John Crow cawed, spread wide his

wings and flew off above the tree line. I jumped into the water fully clothed, neglecting to even remove my notepad and broken pencil. I swam all the way to the far side and back. Then I walked dripping wet up the path and home.

THE CLOTHESLINE DOOR

W. P. KINSELLA

When the Ontario School Librarians Association held its 20th annual conference a few years back, I was privileged to be one of the writers invited to discuss their works and the pertinence of their use in the classroom.

W.P. Kinsella was the keynote speaker at the event. If you're not already familiar with his adult bestsellers, pick up a copy of *The Dixon Cornbelt League* or any of the novels which have won him the Canadian Authors Association Award, the Books in Canada Award and the Leacock Medal. To me, however, he will always be the man who overcame my hatred of sports tales with his *Shoeless Joe* story — later made into the Kevin Costner movie *Field of Dreams*. Not everyone can fuse baseball and the supernatural so seamlessly . . .

A lot of people were vying for his attention after his address, so I just left a timid note describing *The First Time* for him at the reception desk. I wasn't sure it was the proper way to go about this, but I must have done something right, for he sent in the following piece a few weeks later.

Hardcore Kinsella fans take note: this straightforward account of the way things were back in the "good old days" is quite a departure from the man's wilder antics. Then again, if you thought modern times were screwy when it came to sex, you're about to find out that no era has exclusive dibs on this issue.

The Clothesline Door

How times change. Or do they? I now have a grandson about the age I was when my first sexual experience took place. Is he as ignorant as I used to be? I doubt it.

Oh, if there had only been adult videos in the early fifties. I remember a boy bringing a French postcard to school and charging a nickle per viewing. The card was a picture of a rather pretty young woman in black panties and bra, and there was no question that she was unfastening the bra. But that was all.

I grew up an only child in a household where sex was never discussed, where I not only never saw either parent naked, but not even partially unclothed. My sex education occurred in ninth grade, when a blushing teacher skipped over the reproductive section in boys' health class by saying, "You know, that's when rabbits have little rabbits."

Having reached my final year of high

school without knowing there was such a thing as homosexuality, without being able to find even a picture of a naked woman, the best I could do was to study *Gray's Anatomy* at the library where I worked part time, though I found the diagrams essentially unhelpful. I knew women were constructed differently from men, but how differently? I had only the vaguest idea of what the sex act involved.

With that kind of background, it's not surprising that my first serious encounter with sex was a disaster.

My girlfriend, who I'll call Sonja, was two years younger, and no more knowledgeable about sex than I. We began dating after she invited me to a Sadie Hawkins Day party (an event which, I realize, attaches me to an era when dinosaurs still roamed the Earth). Her family lived about two miles away, on an acreage out on the highway. For all intents and purposes, she, too, was essentially an only child, having a sister barely out of diapers and a much older brother who left home when she was a baby.

It must be hard for today's youth to imagine the lack of privacy suffered by past generations. My father had died the previous year, and I lived with my mother and her sister, my maiden aunt — two formidable little women, who were present and awake twenty-four hours a day. Sonja was caught in much the same situation. Her mother and sister were always at home, and her parents never went out except for about two hours on Sunday evening, when they packed her baby sister into the station wagon and visited relatives. Sonja was allowed to stay home to do homework.

Of course, she wasn't allowed to have me over on such occasions. Therefore, I visited at every opportunity. She would phone me as soon as her parents went out – I travelled on foot and there was only one road into town, so it wasn't a good idea to let her folks see me walking in the direction of their home – and I would more or less sprint the two miles to her place, where we would spend an hour or so kissing passionately and doing a certain amount of exploration. Being inordinately responsible, we always stopped far short of the actual act, though.

There was also a problem with my leaving Sonja's house. It was not advisable that her parents pass me walking back toward town. And as with virtually every house in North Edmonton, the front door was never used – in fact, it was painted shut. So, if I couldn't leave before the family returned, I had a choice of possibly being seen rushing up the driveway while they parked the car in the garage or I could use the clothesline door. That was usually what I did.

The clothesline door. Another archaic device, virtually unknown now that even the poorest families have access to a clothes dryer. But back then, in cold climates where -50°F was not uncommon (my hometown certainly qualified), houses were built with back porches, and on the far wall of the porch, a narrow door about four feet tall and a foot wide was cut. One end of a clothesline was anchored indoors, and thanks to the opening, one was able to hang clothes on the line in the relative comfort of the back porch.

So I would be dressed and waiting, and as the car turned into the driveway and headed toward the garage, I would kiss Sonja a final time, squeeze out the clothesline door on the far side of the house and head diagonally across a vacant lot to the highway, completely out of view. Sonja would then shut the door and be in her room by the time her parents entered the house.

We dated for several months and declared our love for each other, but our dates were mainly to movies, plays or school dances, and our time alone was minimal. We did most of our kissing in driveways and behind lilac bushes as we walked the mile from the end of the bus line to Sonja's home.

I bought her a friendship ring, and we decided to become engaged as soon as I graduated from high school and took a full-time job. We rationalized that since we planned to become engaged and would certainly marry in a year or two, it was only logical that we should have sex.

I hardly need to describe the embarrassment of buying condoms, which, in the 1950s, were locked away out of sight, so they cold be kept from the people who needed them most. Some kind of law also stated that when someone wanted to buy them, there would only be a female clerk on duty, usually an older woman who pretended not to hear and made you repeat your request while looking at you as if you intended to rape and dismember her.

She was apt to know you, too. Ah, that's the widow Kinsella's boy, who lives up on 71st Street, and I've seen him riding the bus with Sonja So-and-so, and Sonja's mother attends my church, I'll bet she'd like to know what I've seen.

There was no clerk-client privilege.

So I waited until Saturday afternoon, and then pointedly didn't bring the condoms on our movie date that night – Sonja was highly curious, and I could just see us in the little bus that looked like a cream- and-red cartoon loaf of bread, opening and examining the package all the way from North Edmonton to downtown.

I guess the manufacturers assumed that the condom, like the lever or the inclined plane, was self-explanatory. I'm sure the package contained no instructions. As I recall, the only printing on the back of the carton read FOR THE PREVENTION OF DISEASE. But even if there had been instructions, we probably wouldn't have used them, as I pride myself to this day on never having read the directions accompanying anything.

When I reached Sonja's house on Sunday night (taking longer than usual because a freeze-the-balls-off-a-brass-monkey Alberta blizzard had been raging for two days), she had already changed into a frilly nightgown, which set off her red hair, and she had turned down the covers of her bed. We both mistakenly assumed that once we had rid ourselves of our clothes, instinct would kick in automatically, and we would do whatever it was that nature intended. At that point, however, we just gawked at the condom. We gathered that it was supposed to somehow fit over my penis, but the exact mechanical principle eluded us.

In spite of being naked in bed, we were still responsible. We tried several ways of attaching the condom in place – we did manage to roll it over the head of my penis, but that was as far as we went. It seems impossible that we could have been so inept, yet I remember thinking that even if we did solve that puzzle, I'd still have precious little idea of what would happen afterwards.

Fortunately, Sonja seemed to have a pretty good idea about that part. Unfortunately, the condom refused to stay on, and neither of us proved intelligent enough to handle the mystery.

After a number of unsuccessful tries, Sonja, my penis and I were tired and frustrated, giddy and laughing like the incompetent children we were. We returned to the living room and were just starting to get dressed when the headlights of a car turning into the driveway flashed across the front windows. Her family was home forty minutes early.

I struggled into as much of my clothing as possible, slipped my bare feet into my fleece-lined boots and, carrying my shoes and parka in my arms, charged into the back porch. But the wicked wind of the blizzard had pushed the snow against the house, and the drifts, solidly packed, rose a foot above the bottom of the clothesline door, keeping it from opening properly. I imagined I could hear the squeal of the parents' feet on the ice as they approached the house, and I leapt against the pane with all my might, only to disappear chest deep in the snowbank. Shoes and coat held over my head, I quickly waded away into the bitter wind.

I had left the condoms behind – Sonja returned them to me at school the next morning. But I knew I could never try this again in her bedroom, for my attention would be focused on watching for lights in the driveway. And as I realized that our one opportunity at privacy could be interrupted at any time, it became clear that there was nowhere we could be securely alone.

So, however unwillingly, we ended up postponing any further attempt.

BORDERS

MARTIN STEPHENS

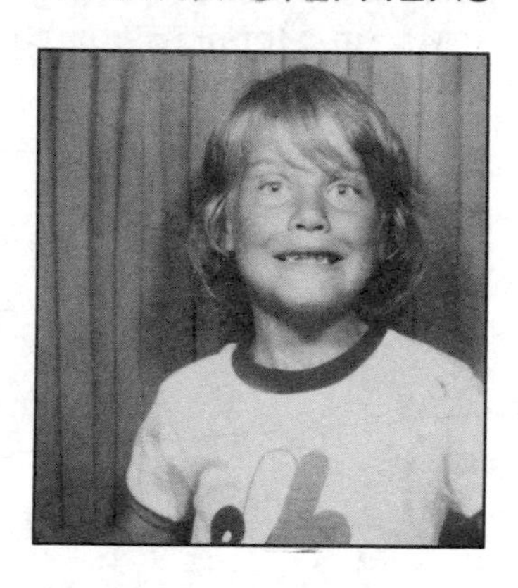

It has long been established that rape has little to do with sex. It's more a matter of power plays, domination, control and outright violence.

Accordingly, you may wonder why we included the following text in a collection of stories about sexual relationships. The rules here just aren't the same, and the confrontation occurs on a very different plane.

Still, try as we might we couldn't pretend that one's first taste of intercourse is always consented to. Incest and child abuse may be universally repulsive, but they happen far too often to be ignored, and we wouldn't have done anyone a favour if we had chosen to look the other way.

Whether we're talking in terms of early milestones or "loss of innocence," such an event will influence one's blooming sex life like no other initiation. And we're very grateful to Vancouver's Martin Stephens for sharing his thoughts on the subject with us.

Borders

The man who used to rape me is dead. I learn of this in a letter from my mother, who mentions it after updating me on the inclement weather and the declining health of her dogs. "I'm sure you'll be sorry to hear that V. has died. He was killed in a boating accident on the weekend." Further details follow, but I've stopped reading. The news sinks in quickly, like a stone dropped in still water. He is dead. Dead. The man I have wanted to kill is now dead.

I can't decide which disturbs me more: the news of his death, or my mother's presumption that I would be sorry to hear of it.

The man who used to rape me is dead. There will be no trial, no investigation, no interrogation. Nothing more will ever come of this. There will be no public acknowledgement that a crime ever took place. Nor will I receive any kind of apology.

I am at once both disappointed and relieved. There was never any evidence to begin with. It would only have been my word against his. And now his words have run out, his voice drowned. Only one version of the truth remains. I may never be proven right, but at least now I can never be proven wrong.

I am free. Free at last. But free from what?

None of this is true, of course.

I am eight years old. I am with my family, walking up Mount Royal. Beside me is my mother; slightly ahead is V. with my brother and sister. We're walking up the path toward the stairs which lead to the lookout at the top of the hill. The leaves are turning colour, so it must be early autumn. I've slowed my step to keep pace with my mother, waiting for V. to walk far enough ahead so as to be out of earshot.

"V. is mean to me," I tell her.

"What?" she asks.

"He's mean to me. He hurts me."

"Nonsense," she says. "How does he hurt you?"

"I don't know. But it hurts." This is the best I can do. I don't have the words for what he does to me. All I know is that it hurts and I want it to stop.

She considers what I've said for a moment, then brings the conversation to an abrupt halt. "Don't be ridiculous," she tells me. "Stop making up stories."

So I do. I stop making up stories. For fifteen years I tell no one else about the abuse. I tell no one about much of anything at all.

None of this actually happened.

I am ten years old. I am sitting on the top landing of the stairs leading to the basement. My mother is below me, standing beside the washing machine. She is bent over the cement laundry sink, oblivious to my presence at the top of the stairs, scrubbing at a small piece of fabric. Her elbows are in furious motion, like the wings of a bird. What she has in her hands is a pair of my underwear, from which she is desperately trying to remove the bloodstains.

She looks up suddenly and realizes I've been watching. For a moment our eyes meet, and I recognize in her face a reflection of my own experience. Behind the fierce denial her eyes betray the damage that she herself has withstood, the abuse she suffered at the hands of her uncle. Abuse which has been passed down from generation to generation like a defective gene.

I think that she might actually have believed it, too, believed that she could wash the entire incident down the drain along with the blood. As long as it all came out in the wash, there would be no reason to make an issue of it.

Mother. How can I ever forgive you for this? Your complicity hurts me more deeply than the abuse itself. You knew. And did nothing. And put me back in this man's care.

You're making all of this up.

I have something to say to the ghost of the man who used to rape me. And to my mother. And to her uncle. And to anyone, in fact, who will listen.

Here is what I have to say, what must be said over and over again until it is heard, until it is believed, until I believe it myself:

This cycle of abuse ends with me. It stops here. It goes no further.

Stop making up stories.
Stop.

It ends as it began: with a dream. The man who used to rape me comes back for me one last time. He is wearing a uniform; at his waist hangs a gun. He is a customs clerk at a border gate. I have just stepped off a plane and am trying to get through. He makes me empty my pockets, to show him what I have with me. I offer him my passport, my wallet. My map. Still he glares at me with his hand out: insistent, dissatisfied. Demanding something that I am unwilling to give. What is it he wants from me? I have nothing left to give him. I have nothing left. I am spent.

He reaches out for me and I feel something stir inside, the slow burn of a dormant longing. I want him to touch me. I want to be held by him, to be held down. I want him to wrap his arms around me and whisper in my ear. I want him to tell me again that everything will be all right, that it won't hurt for much longer, that it will all be over soon.

Guilt washes over me in waves of recognition. This longing is what I have tried so hard to forget, this is what has kept the memories so deeply buried all these years. The truth is that along with the blood and the lies, what took place between us occasionally resembled intimacy. Not only did I allow the abuse to continue, but parts of it I almost enjoyed. This is the true source of my shame: that there was some pleasure mixed in with the pain.

I have never admitted this to anyone. I have scarcely begun to admit it to myself. But only the dead keep their secrets forever.

There. I have named it. Are you satisfied? Now will you let me go?

I reach out to touch him and my hand passes through his flesh as easily as through air. He is gone. Dead and now gone. The border is open. I walk past the gate. I have no map and no currency, uncertain even if I speak the language. Nonetheless I step forward, into an unknown country.

THE ONLY FIRST TIME RACHEL COUNTS

JILL GOLICK

If you've ever wondered what *Sesame Street* writers do in their spare time, this story should be quite an eye-opener.

Yet this is not the first occasion on which Jill has strayed from the beaten path. This exlectic author has put out books on sexuality and AIDS, written columns for the *Toronto Star*, *Teach Magazine*, *Kids Toronto* and *EarthKeeper*, and designed software packages for children – one of which earned her a Parents' Choice Award.

Not enough? Then consider two dozen episodes of the *Foreign Affairs* soap opera, and many more contributions to series like *Shining Time Station*, *Smoggies* and *Street Cents* (and those are just the Ss). If you still want more, see her prize-winning documentary on TV violence, throw in volunteer work for the YMCA, and wrap it up with, uh, "pinball consulting" for feature filmmakers.

In light of all this, the following tale is not as surprising as it might be. The amazing thing is that we actually managed to pry Jill away from all this for more than five minutes.

The Only First Time

Rachel Counts

The last man we'd seen was the pilot of the water plane. He had landed, as you might suppose, on water—Florence Lake, to be exact, deep in the heart of Lady Evelyn Smoothwater Provincial Park. Standing on one of the pontoons, he helped us load our canoes and waited, quite gallantly, I thought, until we had paddled a safe distance away before starting up the props and abandoning us. That was yesterday morning.

Since then, we'd paddled for hours on end. Dip, pull, lift, dip, pull, lift in a neverending rhythm until our muscles ached. Moose waded in the tall grass along the shoreline. Pine clung with tenacity to the outgrowths of rock. There was music in the wind, the cry of the loon and the water giving way to the bows of the canoes. A sense of peace as clear as the air settled on the five of us.

Strength, independence and determination had brought us to this place of beauty. We felt part of it.

Late in the afternoon, we made camp, pitched our tents and cooked chicken, potatoes and corn over the fire. As dusk fell, we squatted on the rocks, washing the dishes and our sticky hands in the cold, velvety water.

"This reminds me of the first time I shaved my legs." Chantal scooped a handful of sand from the bottom of the lake and used it to scour the fire-blackened bottom of a pot. "I was at summer camp and all the eleven-year-olds in my cabin would sit at the edge of the water and shave. It was a ritual."

Lisa yawned and shifted, trying to find a comfortable position for her exhausted muscles. "I was thirteen when I started shaving. This boy named Eddie Franklin kept going on about girls who shaved their legs and wore angora sweaters. My mother absolutely refused to buy me an angora sweater, so I let him go all the way. Right in the basement while she was upstairs playing bridge or something."

"When you were thirteen?" The tin plate Elaine was drying slipped out of her hand, and she had to grab for it quickly before it sank.

"It was my first time."

"Thirteen!"

"So what? How old were you?"

Elaine pulled the plate out of the water and glanced around sheepishly. "Fourteen, but I was an *old* fourteen."

"You guys!" All of Chantal's efforts on the bottom of the pot had done nothing to cut through the black. She passed it to Elaine. "I suppose you were also denied an angora sweater?"

"I'm offended," Elaine snorted. "It was mohair." And then she fell upon Lisa, laughing.

"Do you believe them?" Chantal asked, turning to Rachel and me.

Rachel worked her brush through the mass of frizzy black hair that hung to her shoulders. "How old were *you*?"

"She's still a virgin," put in Lisa.

Chantal sat back against the rocks. "Not quite, but I did save myself for the right man."

"Who?" A chorus of voices.

"His name was Rob."

"Who?"

"You don't know him. It was at camp. All the significant events in my life took place at camp."

"At camp? You couldn't have been that old."

"Almost eighteen. I taught canoeing. Rob taught archery. Neither one of us had campers of our own to take care of. For the first time in my life, I was free – no parents, no supervision."

"So you and Robbie went off into the woods and screwed your brains out all summer long."

"You're a disgusting pig, Lisa," said Chantal. "We spent the whole summer falling in love . . . and necking. Then right at the end of the summer, I decided it was time. I took my toothbrush, and me and Robbie went off into the woods and screwed our brains out."

Evening wore into night. We built up the fire and settled around it in a cosy circle as Elaine told her story, which had nothing to do with mohair, but rather with a cousin from out west whom she'd rarely seen before and hasn't seen since. She won't even go to family weddings lest she have to face him again.

Then I trotted out my tale about the drunken evening when three friends and I picked up a rhythm-and-blues band and took them back to someone's three-bedroom apartment. My girlfriends must have been more experienced than I was, because they managed to snag the bedrooms and the three cutest musicians. I was left with the living room couch and the bass player. Not that it turned out badly. To this day, I'm still rather fond of bass lines.

"Your turn, Rachel," Lisa announced.

Rachel arranged another log on the fire. "Let me think about that."

"What is there to think about?"

"Well . . . I'm not going to tell you about that time by the dock the night of the fireworks. I mean, I was only eleven, and I'm not sure the act itself took place that night. All I really remember is a seventeen-year-old boy I never saw before kissing me and reaching under my clothes and pushing at me in places I'd never been pushed at before . . . So, it doesn't count."

"That was abuse," said Elaine.

"Was it?" It seemed like a new idea to Rachel.

"Yeah, I think so. I mean, he took advantage of you."

"You were a child," said Chantal, firmly.

"Then it definitely doesn't count."

Rachel tried to sound lighthearted. The blackness chilled our backs even as the flames leapt and danced between us. Lisa started to fidget, and I thought she was going to head for her sleeping bag. Rachel's quiet voice stopped her.

"I'm not counting the time with Joe Corelli, either. Even though I *wanted* it to be my first time." Her voice picked up strength and she smiled. "Not that I wanted sex, exactly. Joe did. I wanted a boyfriend. I thought

I could work it to both our advantage."

Elaine snorted. "Fat chance."

"Words of wisdom."

"Learned the hard way."

"We already heard your story, Elaine," Lisa cut her off. She turned to Rachel. "How old were you?"

"Sixteen, I guess. Grade eleven. Anyway, it was way past midnight. We got into his bedroom . . ."

"With his parents home?"

"His parents were never around, even at 3 a.m. Anyway, we're necking and I tell him I'm going to do it this time, so he pulls out the condom he's had ready for about a decade and he tears open the foil and we hear this hammering sound. Someone's pounding on the front door. And the doorbell is ringing." She turns to flash her smile all the way around the circle. "My father."

"Your father!"

Elaine's voice rose above the fray. "How did he know?"

"I never figured it out." Rachel shrugged. "Radar, maybe. I suppose when your sixteen-year-old daughter isn't home and the sun's about up, some instinctual father thing sends you straight to the home of the wildest boy in town. I'm not even sure how he knew where Joe lived."

"What did you do?"

"What we *didn't* do was answer the door. Eventually, he went away and I got dressed and went home."

Lisa was clearly disappointed. "You didn't do it."

"It doesn't count," said Elaine. "You are not getting out of this, Rachel. We want to hear about the first time you *did* do it."

Rachel poked at the fire. "The truth is, I can't remember it."

"Oh, sure." Lisa took the stick out of her hand and did some poking of her own.

"You gotta have a first time," said Chantal. "Don't you?"

"It doesn't make a good story."

"We all told ours."

"You have to tell or . . . " Elaine paused to think of an appropriate threat.

" . . . or we'll make you carry the heaviest pack on every single portage tomorrow," Lisa concluded.

"And there are seven of them," added Chantal.

"Okay, okay," laughed Rachel. "I'll tell you about my first time. The only first time I count. But I have to warn you, I wasn't a virgin."

"Let me get this straight," said Elaine. "You weren't a virgin when you lost your virginity?"

"It's a romantic thing," Chantal explained, breaking into song: "You make me feel brand new . . . "

Rachel grinned. "I'm just setting the stage here. I want you to understand, I'd already tried three different forms of birth control. I'd had sex on two continents. But for me, it all boiled down to lying under some hunk of flesh, staring at the ceiling. I'd start out okay, full of feelings and lust, wanting to get closer and nakeder. I'd be right there with him . . . "

"Who?"

"Whoever. It didn't matter. By the time he was humping away in the throes of ecstasy, I'd be . . . " She tried to come up with the right word. " . . . bored. I'd be bored. The guy was so involved in the moment that he didn't know. And I certainly didn't tell. No way. I wasn't about to let anyone know that I was a freak of nature, a pervert who didn't like sex. So I pretended."

"You faked orgasm?"

"I faked interested. But I was really thinking about my chemistry final or the effects of ozone depletion on birds or something."

"The missionary position isn't optimal for clitoral stimulation," intoned Elaine.

"Now she tells me." Rachel stood up and walked away from the fire. She came back with an armload of wood and tossed a piece on the fire. Lisa used the stick to push it into the centre of the flames.

Rachel settled back into her place. "Then

I found the *Hite Report.* What an amazing book – six hundred pages of women talking about sex! What they like and don't and when, where, how, who. I'd never seen anything like it. I went straight to the section called "Women who Orgasm During Intercourse: How They Do It." This was what I wanted to know. I started underlining frantically – if these women could do it, I was bloody well going to learn.

"But it wasn't just the information that got me excited. There were all these words. Words like *deep* and *thrust. Smooth. Tongue.* The words were having a kind of interesting effect when an entire phrase caught my eye: *women who masturbate.* Women!? I swear to God, I was twenty years old and I didn't know. Women can masturbate. Why didn't I know this?

"I was reading, skimming, rushing through the words. One after the other, these women described exactly what they did, whether they spread their legs or squeezed them tightly together. Up and down or round and round. Fast or slow. Gently or with steadily increasing pressure. One woman used a pencil. I was holding a pencil . . .

"The book fell to the floor. I fumbled with the zipper of my jeans as if I'd never undone them before."

"A pencil?" Elaine looked as if she'd eaten

a lemon. "Tell me you didn't use a pencil!"

"A yellow, six-sided HB."

"Yuck!" Lisa was grinning wide.

"It was not an entirely unpleasant sensation, but I couldn't stop worrying about the metal band that keeps the eraser in place. The mood passed.

"However, I was not about to give up. The next time, I treated myself a little better. Picture this: candlelight, perfume, soft music, a hot tub of bubbles and a bar of expensive French soap. I'm nice and relaxed, lazily running the soap over my skin, down my sides to my hips, my thighs . . ."

"Rachel!"

"Shut up, Chantal. Go on," commanded Lisa.

"The soap was the right shape and just slippery enough. I tried round and round and up and down. Slow and fast. But then all those little drips coming out of the tap would distract me or I'd notice my toenails needed clipping. But I'd bring myself back, try to focus. The feeling was pretty interesting and I thought maybe I would find out what guys feel like. You know what I mean?

"And then a new sensation entered the picture. A kind of soreness. No, rawness."

"Ooo." Elaine's hands fell into her lap.

"The soap," said Rachel. "The wonderful, expensive French soap. It was either the colour or perfume in it that did it. I'm not sure which, but I've never been attracted to soap since.

"It took about a week to recover. The next time, I tried my pillow, lying flat on my stomach, but it was just too flimsy. I took a shot at wiggling against the seam of a tight pair of jeans, but they ripped before much could happen. The doorknob was too high for comfort. And I didn't have the guts to go into a store to buy a vibrator.

"It was pretty frustrating, but the more I tried and thought about it, the more I thought about it and tried.

"So one night in bed, I'm lying there, thinking about all my failures. My hand is on my stomach and it kind of moves to my legs and finds its way between them. I never thought of using my fingers before because I couldn't imagine that touching my own body would be at all interesting. I was wrong.

"Mentally, I listed all my favourite words from the *Hite Report*: Gentle. Damp. Rhythm. Circular. Squeeze. Slow. Slide. Slip. Ah, the power of words.

"It wasn't easy going. I mean, it felt good, but sometimes my mind would wander. What was it supposed to do when my body was otherwise occupied? Review the list of words. Think about what (or who) was to come. Focus. Think. Don't think. Keep the hand moving. Change the motion. Slow, slide, slip. Squeeeeze."

The brilliance of the red and orange flames reflected in Rachel's eyes as she paused. Then a small smile formed on her lips. "That was my first time."

We laughed for a long time. Whenever we managed to get control of ourselves, someone would whisper "slow, slide, slip" or "HB" and we'd all break up again.

It was Lisa who finally brought us back to reality. Rising and stretching, she announced, "It's late and tomorrow is portage city."

We doused the fire, checked that the canoes were secure and straggled toward our tents. Flashlights were turned out one by one. A few crickets chirped and the wind played in the leaves above us. Not far away, the lake lapped at the shore.

I was exhausted from work and air and food and fun. I'm sure we all were. But on that dark, peaceful night in the middle of nowhere, I don't think any of us went right to sleep.

WHITE ON WHITE

CHARLES MONTPETIT

Way back in 1982, I took part in a writers' correspondence workshop. Every second week, the participants had to write a short text on a given theme, and then they would send it to everyone else in order to elicit constructive criticism.

Assignment number eleven called for a romantic yet ridiculous character who'd still manage to earn the reader's sympathy. It sounded simple enough, but no matter what I tried to invent, one of the three ingredients would always be missing. My creations either came across as interesting jerks whose affections seemed forced, decent sweethearts whose silliness was artificial or bumbling lovers whom no one would believe in. Chaplin may have made it look easy, but I had a long way to go.

Then I remembered the most basic of all storytelling rules: if you're concerned about realism, write about something you know intimately. My budding love life immediately came to mind, and since it met all the assigned prerequisites, I summed it up in a bittersweet little piece, expecting this to be the end of my troubles.

It wasn't. First Time stories must be very contagious, for as soon as people heard about mine, I got to hear about theirs. And the more I heard, the more I had to admit there was a book in there somewhere.

And that, children, is how this anthology was born.

White on White

Maybe I shouldn't have thought about it so much. After all, our first encounter was supposed to be a business meeting – and a very short one at that. She was on her way to a cocktail party; she'd said she would only drop in for a second; the motor of her car would be running in the driveway. By any standard, I had absolutely no reason for wondering about our future together.

Then again, I did that with every single woman I met. I was nineteen, I was a virgin, and I felt my clock was running late.

The statistics said so. I had dug up the numbers, and I had found that most people had got their first taste of sex by the time they were through with grade eleven. I was a sophomore at Concordia University. Apparently, I had missed out on something much more important than good marks, and I didn't want it to go on for lack of attention on my part.

But I wasn't horny, if that's what you're thinking. Horniness was the trademark of giggling teenagers in silly beach movies, and its sole focus were the sex kittens that Hollywood insisted on portraying every year. As far as I could tell, real women weren't at all like that, and whether they were oppressed or liberated, lust usually was a bad move to start with. Supportiveness had become the new buzzword; if you wanted anything beyond that, you had to wait for The Sign.

Believe me, I looked for it everywhere, from anyone – and I do mean *anyone*. The girl behind the cafeteria counter. My Communication Arts teacher. The dentist at the local clinic. It may seem extreme, but it wasn't the kind of thing that stood in the way of developing casual friendships. Whenever I met someone new, a part of my mind would simply start listening for special clues and, if it detected any, it would steer me in the appropriate direction.

Then I'd gotten this call from the editor of a small production company. She wanted to use one of the ideas I had sent her for a documentary (something about the nonsmokers' crusade – *The Incombustibles*, I believe it was called). She was quite enthusiastic, which was a turn-on in itself, so when she'd offered to pick up more material that very afternoon, my imagination had kicked into overdrive. *Hey, she may be the One, don't blow this. The industry isn't exactly crawling with nice people who make house calls.*

I had precious little time to think it through, though. The stuff I had written needed a lot of touching up, so I forfeited my Film History class in order to make it more presentable. After all, it was my first sale, and I was terribly eager to please: had she asked for the moon, I'd have included any other planet in the bargain.

I was still slaving away at it when I heard her climb the outside staircase. I lunged for a comb and a manila envelope, the doorbell rang and I braced myself. This, I believed, could be a doubly historic occasion.

I opened the door . . . and for the first time in my life, I thought, *No it isn't.*

It was odd, for I'd never been particularly fussy about people's appearances. I knew looks could deceive, and I didn't want to let physical preferences get in the way of a potential romance. For all intents and purposes, Carole's cheerful assurance had done all the conquering she needed to do over the phone.

Body language, however, was a different issue. Whether she knew it or not, she spoke volumes in that department, all of it against our becoming an item, ever.

It doesn't matter if you're on your way to the poshest reception in town. Alone in the afternoon sun, anyone would look silly in such a pretentious dress, laden as it was with heavy jewellery and noxious perfume clouds. She was tottering on her spike heels, her nails glittered like chrome fireflies and she hardly seemed able to breathe under all that makeup. A self-conscious, artificial smile was plastered on her face, the kind she'd have worn if she'd been trying to borrow a hundred grand from a distant acquaintance. She was bubbly, she was mundane, she was following a clichéd recipe for Making It in High Society.

I just stood there in my faded corduroys and day-old stubble. We obviously belonged to different worlds, so I got off the sex track and handed her my script. I even added a few cartoons I'd made in connection with the project, but she just nodded politely before handing them back. I could see her thoughts were on champagne and canapés, so I cut it short and I watched her go, expecting her to disappear from my life.

Yeah, sure.

She phoned back a few days later. There were blanks to be filled in her documentary and she didn't have enough time to order new visuals . . . but maybe something could be rigged up so my artwork would do the trick. Would I care to come over and discuss it?

Even though my gonads had cooled down considerably at that point, the prospect of a second sale was more than enough to fire my professional interest. I must admit I was a bit dismayed when she gave me an unsavory address in the East End – I had pictured her owning a plush penthouse in the heart of the city – but it was my turn to be courteous, and I said fine, no problem.

As it turned out, my class prejudices were no better than hers. While decrepit buildings did weigh down the area, her street happened to be located in the midst of a beautiful oasis – two blocks' worth of lush greenery, complete with community gardens and one of the city's few outdoor swimming pools. I had been apartment-hunting for a long time, and I fell in love with the place on the spot (I now live on that street, and I've never regretted it).

Carole herself was a greater surprise. She'd apparently walked in a few minutes earlier, and was smuggling week-old dishes out of the living room when I showed up. She had traded her heels for white socks, and she slid to the door in jeans and tousled hair, dark locks thriving every which way like wild wool.

"You weren't supposed to see this mess," she said with an impish grin.

I played along and closed my eyes, letting her laugh lead me to the sofa. I could now see why she tried to put on an act out there in the business world. In private, she could be mistaken for a street-smart kid.

It's not that she seemed very tough. Her figure was small and wiry, her bones thin and her muscles nonexistent, yet she had that race-you-round-the-block intensity which dared you to perform any better than she did. She was constantly on the move, and every few seconds her face would light up with a new expression, her eyes wildly flashing and her mind on computer time, ready to one-up everything you'd care to throw her way.

Once again, our business transaction was expedited in a few minutes. We just spread the drawings on the carpet, and immediately agreed on the ones which suited her purpose.

But the rest of the conversation lasted four hours.

If she had gone into comedy, she would have made a killing. Now, I know that people say this of anyone who can tell a joke, but in her case, you'd have sat down and taken notes. Her timing, her delivery, her comebacks were all impeccable. She had the fire of the all-time greats, and she could deadpan her anecdotes with the harsh impudence of the worst shysters. She'd go from the uses of men's baser instincts to ways in which sizzling miniseries could be generated from any situation, sprinkle this with fascinating tidbits about the private lives of public personalities and then blow the lid off a dozen success stories which would never have worked out if human beings were the least bit intelligent. In short, she told me everything she knew about mass media, and how she managed to love it all in spite of the evergrowing number of people she hated in that particular universe.

When she finally paused to catch her breath, there were no buses left on the streets.

The spell broke. I wasn't rich enough for taxicabs, and the idea of borrowing money on our first "date" was just as repugnant as the prospect of spending the next two hours walking back to my bed.

There was a third possibility, mind you. Carole suggested it.

It sounded so logical, I actually believed staying over was the thing to do. When she unfolded the couch, I was glad to see she could accommodate a guest. And when it became clear that this was her *only* bed, I just thought it was great that she didn't mind sharing.

I quickly slipped under the covers while she brushed her teeth in the bathroom. She came out in her nightgown, turned off the lights, tucked herself in, and I did my damned best to stick to my side of the mattress.

There was a moment of dead silence.

Then she said, "You can touch me if you want."

And I thought, WHAT? IT'S GOING TO BE TONIGHT?

Parachute training, Perris Valley, California. There are only six of us, and I'm beginning to have second thoughts about this bizarre way of spending the holidays.

When we get to choose a jumping order, I figure that my best bet is fourth. Three ahead, two behind, no time to panic; just secure your gaze to the back of diver number three and go with the flow when we file out. First-jump parachutes open automatically, but I'm determined to pull the dummy handle like a pro.

Unfortunately, strong winds force the pilot to make two jaunts above the target. The plane has to get back in position after the first three jumps, so there is a long pause as it circles the entire field.

I end up staying a full minute in the open doorframe.

When the instructor finally yells "Go," I've blanked out everything I learned in the previous hours. I say "Ah" and "Wait a minute" but she just repeats the signal. I can't bring myself to leave, yet I know I should get out of the way – so I step outside.

The thing is, I cannot recall the next instant. From that one step to the opening of the chute, there is a hole in my life. My mind refuses to deal with it.

It just doesn't make sense.

And so it went with my first night at Carole's. I was so convinced that nothing would happen with her that my libido never got switched on – and the punch line caught me totally off-guard. Somewhere in the recesses of my brain, the scene was ruled to be ludicrous, and the whole sequence went back to the studio for editing.

REWIND/ERASE.

The moment I'd waited for since puberty was wiped out.

This wasn't what I'd been told would happen. For years and years, everyone I'd talked to and every book I'd read on the subject had treated the First Time as the most memorable event of one's life. Whether it had gone well or not, it was supposed to stick with you for ages. The memories could always fade a little bit with each replay, or they could keep you traumatized until you learned to deal with them, but they never disappeared so cursorily, as if they were no more significant than a discarded gum wrapper!

True, there may not have been much happening in the first place, for I do remember that I had a tough time finding something to say after the fact. I came up with a lame "I never thought it could be so good," but it didn't mean much. As I was mouthing the words, I was perfectly aware that I was lying through my teeth.

(Not very fair, is it? The sex scene is censored, yet the disappointment, the awkwardness and the lie are very much with me.)

My only other memory is that we both overslept – until loud knocks at the door snapped us back to reality. Carole's business partner was tired of waiting for her in the car. Since they were to have breakfast with their backers in fifteen minutes, could she speed it up a little?

Carole turned into a blur. While I was still shaking the shards of sleep from my head, she had already jumped into a business suit, applied her makeup and gathered the documents she needed for the meeting. She blew me a kiss on the doorstep, and in a mock whisper, told me to lock up when I left. Then she was gone.

I was in a bit of a hurry myself, so I picked up my clothes and made a beeline for the nearest bus stop. I was aware that this had been an important day for me, but I was too dazed to sort my feelings about it. I wasn't complaining, though. Having finally slept with someone other than my kid brother was enough to carry me through most of my morning classes.

We did see each other again, too – about once a week, as if to make sure there *was* something going on between us. Besides, now that the primal urges were out of our systems, we could afford to back-pedal a little bit. You know, get to know each other and all that.

And the more I learned about Carole, the more I wondered *which* of our first two encounters had really been an act.

For one thing, she had been sincere when she'd made all those spiteful remarks about her line of work. She may have hid behind a veneer of cynicism, but she had swallowed the entertainment world's lowest standards and made them hers. Promoting outdated social attitudes had become her true gospel, and her devotion to cheap sensationalism was equalled only by her scorn for any type of women's emancipation, including her own. Wrapped in a gauze of poor self-esteem, she was the first victim of the trashier projects that her own company had to undertake in order to stay afloat.

In fact, her whole life could have matched any of the far-fetched stories that soap operas thrive on. The child of a single parent, she had played the role of surrogate adult for ten years before entering a sexless marriage with a fifty-year-old man – and since he already had a pregnant daughter her age, she'd suddenly faced the prospect of turning into a grandma without having ever been a teen or a mom. At twenty-five, this can seriously mess up your mind. Luckily enough, she was granted a divorce before she went berserk. And ever since that time, she'd tried to recapture both the adolescence and the motherhood that had eluded her.

This, I was to find out, is where I came in.

I wasn't exactly told what my part was. It's just that pills were too chemical. IUDs hurt her. Shields and condoms turned her off. And when I mentioned that the only reliable type of birth control this left me with was a vasectomy, she looked so horrified that I quickly canned the idea.

I don't know what we had done for protection on our first night, but I wasn't sure it should happen again. Honest, I wasn't ready for this.

I said so. To my surprise, she agreed to everything. We decided to wait.

That's when the Sex Wars started.

It was rather simple, a kind of game, really. She'd try to entice me – and I'd try to resist. She would dress up, playact, make all sorts of arousing proposals, and I would tag along, return the favours, introduce ideas of my own, yet stop short of intercourse. If she insisted, I backed off. And if she got angry, pouted or pleaded, I'd either walk out, console or argue.

I knew it was a bit twisted, but aren't all sex acts based on a precarious equilibrium between desire and fulfillment, excitement and release, pleasure and withholding pleasure? Intercourse may be an important part of making love, but compared with the amazing variety of forms that the prelude can take, it can seem a bit limited in the long run. Foreplay, on the other hand, is where the real fun lies. When either partner is creative enough, the erotic tension, in and of itself, can be most enjoyable if you play your cards right.

Of course, I didn't think of it in those terms at the time. I was merely focusing on the pleasant parts while trying to ignore the inconvenient ones. When your first taste of sex comes from someone with whom you can't go all the way, but who will indulge many of your wild fantasies, you try to make the most of it.

Unfortunately, it never lasted very long

– as newcomers to the game, neither of us had developed the required patience. If we had seriously tried to build something in common instead of pulling in our respective directions, we might have achieved some sort of durable truce. As it was, however, we merely piled frustration upon frustration.

And then, all of a sudden, the game became dead serious.

When she called one evening, her voice was bone tired, as if she was running on spent batteries. I tried to make some half-assed remark about the way her job was wearing her down, but she wasn't listening:

"Don't get mad, okay? You won't believe this, but . . . uh . . . well, I did it again."

I didn't catch her drift, and she didn't offer any help, veering off on a tangent as soon as I prodded her for details. But she wouldn't stray very far, either, for she kept making oblique references to an earlier monologue of hers, an hilarious piece of black cynicism in which she'd joked about her attempts to end it all.

Somehow, it wasn't funny anymore.

When I finally got the message, I started shaking like a leaf. She could still command enough authority to keep me from calling an ambulance, so I just said "Hold on," rushed into the street, stopped the first car that came along and asked the driver to take me as far as he could in that direction, please, it's an emergency. Then I ran the rest of the way.

By the time I got there, her slashed wrists had turned yellow-green under the action of some cheap disinfectant, and she was clumsily trying to patch them up with cotton strips and masking tape. There was nothing for me to do but tear up more cloth and help her apply it to the wounds. The bleeding eventually stopped, so the cuts must not have been very deep. We both sighed with relief when the stains stopped showing through the fabric.

And all the while my mind was reeling *this is crazy this is insane I care for her she can't do this we had it nice can't she see it what's wrong with her?*

She may have been sincere in her plea for attention, but she'd chosen the wrong way of going about it. I tried to comfort her with reassuring clichés—I love you, you'll see, we'll work this out, don't worry—but at the same time, I realized that she fed on compassion as mercilessly as a loan shark conducts business. She had bet the farm on this latest attempt to win my sympathy, but she didn't seem to care if it put our entire relationship in jeopardy.

Right then and there, I decided I wanted out.

I couldn't leave her at once, that much was clear. You just don't kick someone who's so vulnerable. Besides, I had never *dumped* anyone before . . . but I'd been dumped often enough to be familiar with the pain it involved, and I wasn't in a hurry to inflict it on someone else.

What's more, that pale smile of hers kept playing havoc with my heart, even though I knew she was dragging me under. This only made me feel more wretched, for I knew I had to be awfully depraved to feel turned on while she lay there on her sullied mattress.

Maybe that's what finally clinched it, a feeling of revulsion for the convoluted state of our relationship. I was mixed up, she was mixed up – and as she was on the rebound from earlier traumas, it was the wrong combination for her to recover in. I decided that I'd get her to broaden her dating habits as soon as she was up for it.

I'm afraid I didn't put my foot down hard enough. Quite frankly, I chickened out: when she finally returned to her ebullient self a few weeks later, I merely hinted that I wouldn't mind it if she spent *some* of her time with other suitors. Hell, I actually suggested a few prospects right off the bat.

Anyone else would have got the message anyway. But she took this to be openness on my part, and I compounded the problem by assuring her I wasn't the possessive type. True, her hitting rock bottom in my company had been a blow to the old ego, but it had also proved that her desires weren't being met. So why not try a looser arrangement? Now that we had sunk this low, we could only go up, right?

Wrong.

Oh, she did go on halfhearted dates with a few guys. But she did it for *my* sake, and it didn't change her plans in any way. Whoever she went out with got a pat on the back, and a "no thanks, I'm seeing someone else at the moment." Indeed, why would she have started over from scratch, when she'd already landed the man she wanted to train for the job?

It was embarrassing, not to mention inefficient. Sometimes, we'd go to parties and we'd both flirt around with strangers, but neither of us would follow through, for fear that the other wouldn't, either. Inevitably, we'd end up leaving together, and everyone would wonder what that little performance had been about.

This might have gone on for a long time, too, but the situation came to a head during a weekend at her stepdaughter's place.

Ironically, Laure was the only person who seemed to have a good handle on my girliend's mood shifts. A sturdy country type with a solid head on her shoulders, she'd laugh off any attempt at emotional blackmail, or bite right back if she felt she was taken advantage of. Still, the two women got along like best school chums, and it made for heady conversation, morning till night.

Laure's cottage was small and far from soundproof, so even when I repaired to another room, I could hear her take my side and get heated up about it. She'd browbeat Carole into admitting that she was the exact opposite of the wreck she pretended to be, and she'd get her to take stock of everything she had going for her, come on, once more without the bull. This guy is one of the good ones, why are you taking your crap out on him?

I didn't want to let her do all of the job, though, so when Carole said she'd try to improve, I joined in and said I'd do my part, too, the moment she started to clean up her act.

I guess it shows how little I knew about these situations. I'm not sure Laure rolled her eyes when I spoke up, but I definitely shouldn't have said that.

The next day, Carole was given a new lease on life. She helped with the house chores, she ate with renewed appetite, she grinned and joked for hours on end. We played with Laure's baby and she didn't [illegible] sad. We trekked through the woods and it w[illegible] flawlessly romantic. You could have sworn[illegible] she was enjoying it all.

When we finally retired to our room, she seemed mightily pleased with herself.

"Was I good?" she asked with a triumphant smile.

"Very much so," I said, only to realize that I had just painted myself into a corner. Her eyes were pleading again. She didn't have to spell it out; what she expected from me was plain as day.

Pay up.

After all, she'd kept her end of the bargain. If I was the gentleman I pretended to be, I couldn't renege on my pledge – why would I have asked for her word if I felt free to break mine? A promise was a promise, it was as simple as that.

"But it's only been one day," I protested.

"So? I'm asking for a few minutes in return. You're off easy."

"It's not the same. What you want is major."

"And a complete personality change isn't? Thanks a lot."

"How do I know you weren't just pretending?"

She looked genuinely outraged. "Hey, are we going to trust each other or not? You're one who's waffling, so I've got more ...asons to doubt *your* sincerity."

"You can't rush someone into this. It takes time."

"It takes two, as well. Am I supposed to be this good little girl for six months and then let you decide *if* I get a reward? I think I'm entitled to a downpayment, and I want it now."

So this is what romance is all about, I thought. Two stones rubbing each other until one is worn away. Passion is reduced to persistence: you give in when your strength runs out, and the winner gets to screw the other one. No wonder newcomers don't fare too well. They're still waiting for the elusive "spark" while they're being swallowed whole.

I caved in, dammit, and I'm not proud of it. That's my *real* first time, the one I'll remember for the rest of my life: no foreplay, no sweet talk, just the slow grind of reluctant gears. We made love like the actors in a movie, following the script and keeping our hearts shut. A trick of the light on a blinding screen, virgin bodies on immaculate sheets.

It lasted ten, maybe fifteen minutes. The only surprise was that I pulled out just after she'd come, and ejaculated on the bedspread.

There was this shocked look on Carole's

face, as if I had cheated her out of a chestful of doubloons. This time I stood my ground, and made it clear that we'd already done way too much by reasonable security standards. She argued about the point of it all, she said I deprived her of the very sensation she'd looked for. I said it was too bad, but there didn't seem to be enough room left for compromise.

She started crying, and the night ended in sullen silence.

We didn't break up on the spot, but the subject of sex never came up again. We did attend a few more parties together, but it wasn't until I saw her cling to another guest that I knew our relationship had truly come to an end. For a moment, I even felt a pang of jealousy — until it dawned on me that this was exactly what I had wanted in the first place.

We parted ways with a shrug. The entire episode had become unimportant.

I last saw her in the fall, when I sold off my old records in a secondhand store. She now owned a plush penthouse in the heart of the city, her husband was the sweetest, most exciting broker she'd ever met and, as her rotund belly demonstrated, she was in the very last week of pregnancy. I said it was neat. Could she now afford to pay me for my script? She dropped the subject, and offered to drive me home.

Yes, I've thought of counting the months, and I'm pretty certain the dates don't match.

But I don't want to make sure, either.

SO, TELL ME

JULIE LAWSON

Like most of the writers who were approached to contribute to this anthology, Julie Lawson initially thought, "No Way!"

But the invitation brought memories of her old diary back to the surface, and she decided to dig it up and do a little rereading. She still didn't plan on writing a piece, but then, after completing a major project, she found herself driving back to Sooke (British Columbia), and just like she always does when she's on the road, she started to work out the beginning of a story in the back of her mind.

When she got home, that story somehow wormed its way onto a few sheets of paper, and all of a sudden Julie was thinking, "Why not?"

Why not, indeed? As you can probably tell from her prize-winning picture book *The Dragon's Pearl* and her Sheila Egoff Award-honoured *White Jade Tiger* (among other publications), Julie loves time travelling, even if it's just a step into the recent past.

So let's have a toast to the voyages that made this piece possible, and let's join her now on her latest journey.

So, Tell Me

March 25, 12:35 a.m.

Dear Diary,

I DID IT!

The first part was every single word for *wonderful.*

The second part?

Well, the earth didn't move.

Waves didn't crash against the shore.

Fireworks didn't explode. (But we *did* see a shooting star. Which I took to be a sign.)

So where do I start? Maybe with the nuns.

I haven't written about the nuns before. When it happened, I just wrote "The strangest thing happened to me last night. I could never write it down but I'll remember it forever."

I know I wrote those exact words because I looked it up in an earlier diary. May 22, proof positive. I don't know why I didn't fill in the details. Afraid someone might read it, I guess.

I was at home when it happened, right here, asleep in my bed with the chrysanthemum quilt. Suddenly, nuns were in my room. I don't know where they came from. I mean, it's not like I live in a convent. But somehow they appeared, hovering over my bed, draping the bronze and gold chrysanthemums with their long black habits.

And I started to melt. A slow melt. I felt a deep throbbing where I'd never felt throbbing before. I lay without moving, as each throb peaked to a delicious sharpness. Then started again.

It went on for a long time. When it ended, I was awake and the nuns were gone.

I found myself curled up in my usual position. Left side, knees bent, one leg on top of the other, hands by my pillow.

So how did it happen?

I've heard of the Immaculate Conception. Was this an Immaculate Orgasm? If so, I wondered, how do I get another one?

And why nuns? I never knew a nun. I'm not even Catholic.

1:20 a.m.

I tried to sleep, but couldn't. So here I am again.

Before I get into the exquisite details of March 24 – the digits add up to six, my lucky number! – I have a confession. When the Immaculate Orgasm happened, I didn't know about orgasms. Well, okay, I knew the word. It's in my thesaurus between *organ loft* and *orgiastic*. But way back then, I didn't know how an orgasm happened. I thought it was a guy thing.

I wanted to talk to Melanie about it, but I was afraid she'd laugh. Like she did the first time Wayne kissed me. The very next day she'd rushed over and said, "Hey, Caroline! What happened after the dance? You and Wayne took an awfully long time getting to the pizza parlour."

"We were walking."

"I *know* that! But what took you so long?"

"We stopped."

"So? TELL ME!"

A blush crept up my neck and over my cheeks. "He kissed me."

"He *did*?" Melanie squealed. "Where?"

"Outside Morris Electric, you know that light – "

"Not THAT! I mean WHERE?"

"On the mouth." My first kiss. February 15. One plus five equals six. *Hugely* significant.

After the Valentine's Dance, Wayne had suggested we walk to the pizza parlour instead of driving with the others, even though it was raining. We held hands, talking about nothing, giggling about everything. I kept sneaking looks at him, his hair glistening with rain, the smile crease along his cheek, the school scarf bunched up around his neck. "What?" he said, catching me.

"Nothing."

He laughed and squeezed my hand. And when we got to Morris Electric he kissed me.

"So tell me," Melanie had prodded. "How was it?"

"Great! But – "

"What? Come on, I always tell you everything."

"I don't think I did it right."

Melanie hooted with laughter. "How could you do it WRONG?"

"I don't know! I just – never mind."

"Believe me," she said. "There's no wrong way of doing it, as long as you open your mouth. Did you do that?"

"Uh huh," I said lamely.

But Melanie knew better. "You didn't, did you? Honestly, Caroline. Don't you know ANYTHING?"

That's why I didn't tell her about the nuns.

Anyway, I know all about it now. Orgasms and kissing properly.

No thanks to Wayne, though.

After the Morris Electric kiss, Wayne kind of ended. Like there was a short circuit somewhere that went *ffzsspt.* I cried for days. I kept thinking if I'd kissed him properly, maybe he would have kept liking me. It doesn't matter now. It did then – until I realized I wasn't going to die of grief.

There were others after Wayne. Other guys, other kisses, duly recorded in three years of diaries.

And now, there's Martin.

Whew. Time for a break.

1:50 a.m.

I've just come back from the kitchen where I helped myself to four Oreos and a glass of Bailey's Irish Cream that Mom keeps for special occasions. I'd kill for a roast beef sandwich, carnivore that I am. The refried beans keep repeating.

Anyway.

The first time I saw Martin was recorded, of course, in an earlier diary. Remember? Six months, two weeks and five days ago. It was September 6 – that number again – the first day of classes. He came into Psychology and sat right beside me. I like to think it was because he was irresistibly attracted to me, but the truth is, he came in late, glanced around, saw an empty seat that was easy to get to and took it. Maybe Fate played a hand.

The first few classes, I caught myself staring at Martin's hands. Big hands, tanned and smooth, with long, slender fingers. I figured my whole hand would fit inside his palm. I imagined his fingers curling around it, tucking it in.

By Christmas, we had held hands through several movies, gone canoeing and hiking and beachcombing, passed notes through hours of classes and said "I love you" in all ways but one.

So it's no wonder my New Year's Resolution was to take the plunge and get The Pill.

Without telling Mom, I made an appointment to see Dr. Morgan (the first person to have seen me, at three seconds old). When he asked how I was, I cleared my throat and mumbled, "Um, my boyfriend and I have become intimate and I don't want to get pregnant."

I can't believe I said that. *Intimate*. Why couldn't I have bravely said, "My boyfriend and I are going to Have Sex"?

Instead of handing over a prescription, Dr. Morgan explained that since he was

Catholic and didn't believe in birth control, he would have to send me to someone else. So two hours later I'm in the office of another doctor, who got off on this show-and-tell tangent with condoms and diaphragms and charts and models of appropriate body parts and wordy explanations of what went where and how. I finally managed to say, "Thanks, I'll take the pill."

Which reminds me. I'd better take today's.

2:20 a.m.

I can't believe I'm still awake. Can Mom and Dad hear me, I wonder? Will they *know*?

Tonight, on the way home, Martin talked about getting a place of his own, maybe moving to his family's cabin, since no one uses it but him. Maybe next month, after our final exams. He asked me to move in with him. I think it might be time.

I still remember how shocked I was, the first time he took me to the cabin.

"Why?" Melanie had asked, when I told her.

"It's all, well, *bed*."

"How can it be all bed?"

"Because it's a one-room cabin with an alcove, about two metres square. And built into the alcove is the bed. Not a regular bed; it's built on sliding drawers and instead of a headboard there's a window that goes right up to the ceiling. And wherever you go, you see it. Whether you're by the fire or at the table or at the kitchen sink – there's the bed."

"Sounds good to me," said Melanie.

Okay, I admit it. After the first few trips to the cabin I got used to the bed. I even looked forward to it.

Lying there, we could curl up in the quilt and look out at the sea and the sky. We've watched seals popping up in the bay, and great blue herons standing motionless at low tide. We've seen sunsets in colours I've never heard of, and one day we saw a rainbow.

In January, icicles hung from the eaves. For once the West Coast wasn't green and drizzly. It was white with snow and the pond behind the cabin was frozen. So on January 30 we skipped our afternoon classes and went skating.

The pond was enclosed by white woods and blue sky, like a scene in a snow globe, the kind you shake at Christmas. We skated circles around each other and raced across the pond, hearing only the swish of blades on ice. We glided in figure eights, laughing at how red our cheeks were getting, and how our eyelashes tickled with frost.

Back in the cabin we lit a fire, then tumbled onto the bed to warm up. We lay under the quilt, arms around each other, and kissed. Slowly, slowly, Martin's hand moved, over my clothes and underneath, until it was too hot for clothes. His hand explored my body, finding its way over dips and hollows, curves and peaks. I shivered as he traced the inside curve of my arm, the backs of my knees, the stretch of inner thigh. And then he was touching me where I'd never been touched before.

His hand moved in slow, patient circles. Around and around—that's all I could think of. Not fire, not ice, not the possibility of getting stuck in a snowdrift on the way home. Every nerve ending focused on that one spot. I felt it rise and swell under the pressure of his hand. Around and around until it was the dream again, the Immaculate Orgasm, only this time it was definitely hands-on.

"Oh, god," I gasped. My body jackknifed again and again. Poor Martin, he must have thought I was having convulsions.

Then I started to laugh. Not because it was funny, but because I needed the release.

Martin laughed, too. "Wow! Did you come or what?"

I must have given him a blank look because he said, "You know, *come*. Get off. Climax. Whatever."

"Yeah! I guess I had one of those whatevers!"

"Must've been a good one."

"The best," I said. And all the way home, even while I helped dig the car out of the snow, I was thinking – how did he know what to do? Who taught him?

But by the time I got home, I didn't care.

2:53 a.m.

Time to relive the BIG MOMENT.

Martin's New Year's Resolution was to become a vegetarian. You'd think it was a religious conversion, he's been so fanatic about it. Anyway, before we got serious about studying for our final exams, he decided to take me to the cabin and cook me a vegetarian dinner.

So at 4:00 p.m. on March 24 (almost eleven hours ago) he met me outside the library and off we went to the cabin. I daydreamed by the window while he rustled up his gourmet burritos. They were delicious, especially with extra-hot salsa.

After dinner we sat on the beach, watching the stars appear. Water lapped the shore. The harsh croak of a heron made us look up, and we listened to the swoosh of its wings as it flew across the bay. When fog crept in, we snuggled closer. Soon all the stars were hidden.

Inside, we sat by the fire and talked until we ran out of words. Then we just sat, gazing at the flames, gazing at each other in a warm, comfortable silence. And the fullness I felt had nothing to do with refried beans or avocados.

"It's getting hot," Martin said after awhile, taking off his sweater.

I nodded, then raised my arms as he lifted my sweater and gently guided it over my head. One my one, he undid the buttons on my shirt, his eyes never leaving mine until he slipped the shirt off my shoulders. He brushed his hands over my breasts, his touch soft as rainwater. "Do you want to — "

"Yes." I could hardly speak. Across the bay, the foghorn moaned.

He took my hand and led me to the bed. We took off the rest of our clothes and stretched out under the quilt, skin against skin. Our hands whispered over shoulders and breasts, stomachs and thighs, back and front. His hands drew circles over my body until I melted, and came.

After I caught my breath, I said, "Do you want — "

"Yes."

I stroked him, marvelling at how hard he was, and how big, and thinking — it's really going to happen. Tonight I'm going to do it. *We're* going to do it. And we'll both come at exactly the same time, because when *he* comes, it's going to trigger off a gigantic orgasm, just like the hands-on one, only better.

I gasped when he went in.

"Sorry," he said.

"It's okay." The twinge passed. Then he slid in easily, straight to the small of my back. Joining us together like two pieces of a jigsaw puzzle.

And I hugged him, moved with him, waiting for it to happen, anticipating all the words for wonderful –

Suddenly, Martin was rolling onto his side. "What's the matter?" A tight knot formed in my stomach. "Did I do something wrong?"

He smiled and kissed the top of my nose. "Hardly."

"Then why – "

"I came, that's all."

"But I thought – "

"What?" He drew me closer, concerned.

"Nothing," I said. "It doesn't matter." I kissed his cheek and curled up against him, laying my head in the hollow beneath his shoulder, feeling his heart beat under my hand.

So there's a difference between inside and outside. So now I know.

And now I think it wasn't a matter of first part and second part, better and worse, right and wrong. Every moment was part of the whole.

And now it's 3:27 a.m.

Time to sleep.

March 25, 11:00 p.m.

Dear Diary,

No one knew. When I got up this morning, Mom said, "Did you and Martin have a good time at the cabin?"

I couldn't believe it. She had to *ask*? I figured it would be written all over my face.

Dad said, "You two must've woken up the whole neighbourhood last night. When's Martin going to get that muffler fixed?"

Like Martin hasn't got other things on his mind.

Melanie was already at the library when I got there. I sat in the study carrel beside her and waited. *She'll* know there's something different about me, I figured. Melanie with her X-ray eyes and finely tuned sex sense.

I was right. After seven minutes (I couldn't believe her restraint), she leaned over and whispered, "You're glowing."

I nodded.

"So how was it? Romantic? Disappointing?

Did it hurt? Did it take long? Just answer yes or no."

I smiled and said nothing.

"Come on, tell me! Did you like it? Aren't you going to say anything?"

I skimmed over the headings of my Psych notes. Motivation, Perception –

"Give me one word, just one."

I put my finger to my lips. Melanie would have to find her own word.

AND NOW, A SPECIAL INVITATION . . .

I'm sitting in the dark, enjoying the cool night air and a well-deserved rest after a rather harrowing lecture tour.

In walks my stepson Dominic, whose karate class has just ended. He's taller than I am, but he still goes for high vantage points, so he perches himself on the corner of the kitchen counter and we start shooting the breeze for a while.

"So how was the tour?"

"Can't complain. Feels good to be back, though. I've just managed to line up enough contributors for *The First Time,* so I'll be concentrating on that from now on."

"Uh-uh. Well, if you ever need one more writer, I guess I've just become eligible."

"Thanks." [Double take.] "Say *what*?"

"Ah . . . don't tell Mom yet, but Isa and I, we finally made it. It was fabulous."

"Details! I want details!"

Isn't it always the way? As Julie Lawson pointed out in the preceding pages, getting people to discuss how, when and where their First Time took place may not always be a piece of cake, but once the subject is broached, it will not be dropped easily. I should know: in the four years since the original French-Canadian edition of *The First Time* was published, the issue has generated an endless number of fascinating conversations, this anthology being just one of the end results.

Yet the conversations needn't stop here: if your curiosity has been piqued but you couldn't find the angle that you would most have liked to see in our pages, feel free to fill the void by sending us your own stories! If we get enough interesting submissions, we might just put out a sequel to these first two volumes.

The rules are simple:

1) The stories must be about a first sexual experience (no crushes, puppy loves or fantasies). The definition of a

"first time" is left to each individual – but it must be a significant step in one's sexual awakening.

2) The stories must be true (no fiction, hearsay or composite characters). Artistic licence is allowed to modernize the tales or avoid pedestrian details, but the most important facts must be authentic.

3) Self-censorship must be low (you are not required to use euphemisms and circumvent explicit details, but absolute frankness is not a *must*, either). The way one speaks with intimate friends is best.

4) Any length is fine (but the average might hover around ten pages or so). Please type your manuscript in double-spaced format, with one-inch margins all around.

5) There is no deadline. Submissions will be considered on an ongoing basis.

We are presently working on a series of international editions, so the stories do not necessarily have to take place in Canada. And though we're wide open to all kinds of experiences, we're particularly interested in "ordinary" situations, whether they end on a positive or a negative note. A well-written First Time need not be earth-shattering to capture people's attention.

The selected contributors will receive advances and royalties based on book sales, in keeping with the standards generally recognized by professional authors.

If you have any questions, just send us a note, along with a self-addressed, stamped envelope – or, if you live outside of Canada, an international reply coupon.

Our address:

Charles Montpetit
The First Time, volume 3
c/o Orca Book Publishers
Box 5626, Station B
Victoria, BC Canada
V8R 6S4

In the meantime, I'll see if I can get Dom to write his own story.